Wish he was you

Published by © KD Robichaux
Wish He Was You
Copyright © 2015 KD Robichaux
All rights reserved
https://www.facebook.com/authorkdrobichaux

Edited by: Becky Johnson with Hot Tree Editing
http://www.facebook.com/hottreeediting

Cover Photography by: Matt Trevino Photography
https://www.facebook.com/mtrevinophotography

Cover Design © Sommer Stein
with Perfect Pear Creative Covers
https://www.facebook.com/PPCCovers

Formatted by: Author JC Cliff
https://www.facebook.com/BLYSS.TRILOGY

Chapter Headings Designed by: Author Danielle Jamie
https://www.facebook.com/AuthorDanielleJamie

COPYRIGHT

All rights reserved. No part of this publication may be reproduced, stored in retrieval system, copied in any form or by any means, electronic, mechanical, photocopying, recording or otherwise transmitted without written permission from the author/publisher, except by a reviewer who may quote brief passages for review purposes. This book is licensed for your personal enjoyment only. This eBook may not be resold or given away to other people. If you would like to share this book with another person, please purchase an additional copy for each recipient. Thank you for respecting the hard work of this author.

The Blogger Diaries Trilogy, is based on a true story. I have tried to recreate events, locales, and conversations from my memories of them. In order to maintain their anonymity, in some instances, I have changed the names of individuals and places. I may have changed some identifying characteristics and details such as physical properties, occupations, and places of residence.

FBI Anti-Piracy Warning: The unauthorized reproduction or distribution of a copyrighted work is illegal. Criminal copyright infringement, including infringement without monetary gain, is investigated by the FBI and is punishable by up to five years in federal prison and a fine of $250,000.

Except for the original material written by the author, all songs, song titles, lyrics, book titles, movie titles, and excerpts mentioned in this novel are the property of the respective songwriters, authors, and copyright holders. All lyrics belong to the artist and their copyright holder. All reasonable efforts have been made to contact the copyright holders to include in **The Blogger Diaries Trilogy,** and anyone who believes their copyright to be infringed is welcome to contact the author. Except for the original material written by the author, all songs, song titles, lyrics, book titles, movie titles, and excerpts mentioned in this novel are the property of the respective songwriters, authors, and copyright holders.

The Blogger Diaries Trilogy

STOP! STOP! STOP! STOP!

PLEASE, FOR THE LOVE OF COFFEE, DO NOT START READING THIS BOOK WITHOUT READING BOOK 1, *WISHED FOR YOU*, FIRST.

These books are NOT standalones and must be read in order.

Reading order:

Wished for You
Wish He Was You
Wish Come True

Now that I've had a panic attack thinking about someone reading this book first, you may proceed, but only if you've READ BOOK ONE FIRST!
Love,
KD

Preface

You're gone and I gotta stay high
All the time to keep you off my mind, ooh ooh
High all the time to keep you off my mind, ooh ooh
Spend my days locked in a haze,
Tryin' to forget you, babe, I fall back down
Gotta stay high all my life to forget I'm missing you

Staying in my play pretend
Where the fun ain't got no end
Oh, can't go home alone again
Need someone to numb the pain
Oh, staying in my play pretend
Where the fun ain't got no end
Oh oh can't go home alone again
Need someone to numb the pain

~Tove Lo "Habits (Stay High)"

PROLOGUE

Two days.

What it took to pack up my stuff at my brother Mark's house.

Four days. How long it took me to drive from Houston back to Fayetteville, North Carolina.

Two Days. The amount of time I spent in Florida with an old booty-call, halfway through my long drive across the country, trying to desperately fuck the memory of Jason out my head. Because, you know, the best way to get over a guy is to get under another one, right?

Nine days since I got back home, and I've already found the perfect replacement.

Chapter One

Kayla's Chick Rant & Book Blog
May 28, 2005

I went to a party last night with a guy I met on MySpace. His name is Carson, and he's in the Air Force. When I met him in person after messaging back and forth with him for a couple of days, I could tell we weren't a match, but he was still pretty fun to hang out with. He invited me to a house party across town, which was being thrown by one of his fellow Airmen, saying there was going to be a bonfire and drinks. Something about a kegorator...whatever the hell that is.

So, I put on my makeup, did my hair, and dressed in some jeans and a cute black tank top, feeling empty, just as I have for the last two weeks. When I looked in the mirror, all I saw was a hollow vessel staring back at me. The same green-eyed girl I've always been, but I could see the spirit had gone out of them, replaced with a desperation, a need to hurry up and fill the void left behind by the man I knew I was meant to be with, but who threw me away like one of his cigarette butts.

When will these miserable feelings go away? Advice for getting over terrible breakups welcome in the comments.

***

One, two, three. One, two, three, drink.

Last Night

I drove onto Pope Air Force Base after getting my car searched, since I'm a civilian, and met Carson at his dorm room. It's weird calling it a dorm, instead of barracks like the Army base right next door. I've been in a couple of barracks rooms, but never a dorm room. But as I entered the small, colorless, perfectly clean room, containing only a bed, a couch, a TV, and lots of camouflaged stuff, with a tiny bathroom off to one side, I saw it was like all the others I'd seen.

I sat on his couch as Carson finished getting dressed, pulling on a grey T-shirt over his close-cut blond hair, and laughed when I was supposed to at the witty jokes he was making about the people I was going to meet. I think he was trying to loosen me up, make sure I wasn't nervous going to a party where I wouldn't know anyone. But what he didn't realize was I'd been through this before. A few months ago, I was a small-town girl in a big city, who didn't know a single soul or place to go, and found refuge with a couple of strangers who took me in...became my world...made me love them.

Maybe I could do it again. Maybe that was just my trial run, teaching me to be adventurous and open to finding new friends in uncharted territory. Maybe this time, it wouldn't end in heartache; it could heal me.

After he spritzed on too much cologne, we walked down to his giant, white diesel-fed truck, and he opened the door for me. All the while, I was thinking, *Compensating!* as two giant black exhaust stacks stood tall right behind the cab like massive phallic symbols, and I rolled my eyes.

We drove off the base with him blasting country music —*my favorite, not!*—and down the long, empty road that leads to the town on the opposite side of Ft. Bragg from Fayetteville called Spring Lake. There's seriously nothing out there except for a Food Lion.

We turned into a neighborhood of doublewides, and I tried not to show my growing wariness as we pulled into a driveway containing about six or seven other vehicles. I reminded myself these were military people. Any military friends I'd had in the past who lived off base spent the least amount they could on rent so they could spend the rest of their money on toys. And sure enough, as we walked through the squeaky screen-door after climbing the rickety wooden steps, I saw every gaming console on the market attached to a sixty-inch monster of a TV lining one wall of the living room. Unmatched, threadbare furniture sat in a semicircle facing a teenager's wet-dream of an entertainment center.

I followed Carson into the kitchen, where a few people sat around a scratched-up wooden dining table with all different seats, including one black leather computer chair and a bar stool, along with a couple of metal folding chairs. In the center of the table was a bottle of black liquor...like, the liquid was actually black, and to my horror, the only thing sitting next to it was a bottle of apple juice. Just the thought turned my stomach.

"The hell are you drinking, Kyle?" Carson asked, disgust evident in his voice.

"It's called Tattoo. It wouldn't be so bad if I had something besides apple juice to mix it with. One shot, and I already feel like I'm going to ralph," a very attractive guy with brown hair and a little stubble replied from where he was parked in the computer chair.

"Why don't you get your lazy ass up and go get something else to mix it with then?" Carson questioned, slapping Kyle's shoulder as he made his way around the table to what looked like a mini fridge with a tap attached to the top. He pulled down a mug from one of the cabinets and started filling it with golden liquid.

Ah, must be the kegorator.

"Too drunk. I need to hurry up and get off leave. This whole drinking all day thing is going to kill my liver soon," Kyle said, a slight slur to his words.

"I'll drive you," a pretty brunette, with a similar tall, slim build as my own, offered.

"Maybe in a little while. Waiting for the pizzas to be delivered," he told her, and I saw her nod before turning back to the computer she was on in the corner of the room.

"Everyone, this is Kayla. She just moved back here from Texas. She was there for college, but grew up here," Carson announced, and I felt my face grow warm as everyone turned and looked at me. They all offered me warm welcomes, probably used to new people coming to hang out with them, since there's always a steady flow of bodies in and out of the area we live. It's not a common thing to ask someone where they're from, and they say Fayetteville. Being a military town, they're usually just stationed here for a few years before moving on to their next base. Also, with all the training they do at Ft. Bragg, people come for short stints of time for different schools.

"Goddamn it, I can't get this stupid shit to work," the girl at the computer growled, and I saw she had the page opened up to MySpace. Everyone else ignored her, carrying on with their own conversations, so I made my way over to see if there was anything I could help her with.

"What are you trying to do?" I asked, and she turned her

head to the side and up to look at me over her shoulder.

"There's supposed to be a way you can change the background on your profile, but I can't figure out how," she said, banging on the keyboard.

"Oh, I can do that for you. I just did it to my own profile a few days ago. Took me a while, but I finally got it."

She moved out of the seat and opened her hand toward it, offering it to me. I sat down and asked, "Have you found the background you want already?"

"Yeah, this one," she replied, leaning over me to grab the mouse as she clicked on the other tab she had open. She pointed to a brightly colored abstract image, and I showed her how to copy the code and then paste it into her profile. After saving it and going to her page, we saw it had worked.

"Awesome, thank you so much. I was about to throw the damn thing." She laughed and took a sip from her beer bottle that was sitting next to the computer. "I'm Brittany. What's your name again?"

"Kayla. I'm glad to see there's another chick here. I was kinda worried it'd be just me with a shitload of dudes."

"Even if it was, these are all good guys. It's usually just me with all of them. My boyfriend and I live here, but he's deployed right now." She turned to face the room and started pointing out different people. "Kyle lives a few houses down. I actually moved down here with him from Ohio when we were together, but we broke up. We're still best friends though."

She gestured to another guy sitting at the table, who looked like he was concentrating really hard on whatever he was messing with in his hands. "That's Mike. He lives here too. He's really sweet and has a new obsession with rolling his own cigarettes." I glanced over and saw Carson sitting next to him, clapping him on the back and making him spill some of the tobacco he was working with. Mike elbowed him and called him a fucker.

"Oh, I think Carson told me about him. That's his best friend, right?" I questioned.

"Yep, those two are inseparable. They make an odd couple, don't they?" She snorted.

They did look sort of mismatched. Carson was tall, thickly built with blond hair that was almost white. Mike, on the other hand, was tall, but thin and lanky, with hair so dark it was almost black.

They remind me of another pair of best friends.

I shook off the thought quickly and concentrated on what Brittany was saying as she gave me the rundown on the rest of the people standing around the kitchen, and off to the side in what looked like a den, and when I looked toward the living room, I saw more people had shown up and were booting up one of the game systems.

"Jeez, how big do these parties usually get?"

"So big you won't be able to fucking move, and then it starts spilling into the backyard, where we have the bonfire barrel. It was annoying at first, because this is a weekly thing, but with Chris gone, it's kind of comforting having everyone here all the time, and I've learned to sleep through all the noise," she explained. "Here, let me show you around."

She took my arm and pulled me through the growing mass of men, all of them either with a glass or mug full from the kegorator, or bottles they had brought themselves. She guided me through the den and into a hallway with several doors leading off it, walking to the very end so we could work our way back. Opening the last door on the left, she told me it was Mike's room. The walls were covered floor-to-ceiling in Native American art. Even his bedspread had a white wolf howling at a full moon.

Brittany snickered and shook her head at the look on my face. "He's a special one."

The next door on the right was revealed to be the bathroom, and the one next to Mike's room was another bedroom. It had been another roommate's, but they recently got stationed at another base. The final door we came to on the right was Brittany's room. When she opened the door, it was like walking into a completely different world. She had painted the walls a cheerful lavender, with brightly colored accessories around the room, but on one wall, I was surprised to find a massive poster of Chingy. The rapper's presence didn't seem to fit the girly atmosphere or the cute chick who was showing me around the house. The poster must be her boyfriend's.

"You said you live her with your man, right?" I asked, and she looked up from fixing her bangs in the full-length mirror attached to the wall by her door to see me examining the poster.

"Yeah, he hasn't seen the room yet. I did it right after he deployed. I figured if he didn't like it when he got back, at least I'd get to enjoy it for six months before he changes it. That's my baby-daddy." She pointed up at Chingy.

I turned to see her grinning back at me through the reflection in her mirror as she applied some lip-gloss. "Ah, mine is Jared Leto. I would lick that man's skin off," I confessed, making her laugh loudly.

I've never really had close girlfriends, just my Anni, who I have seen every single day since I've been back home, her not wanting to leave my side. She was worried about me, and probably for good reason. I unloaded everything on her that had happened with Jason that last night, and had cried myself to sleep with her arms wrapped around me at her apartment, her trying to make me laugh by explaining in great detail what she was going to do to him after 'flying her ass to Texas.' Made me glad I'm on her good side, that's for sure.

But as I shot the shit with Brittany in her room, it felt like I'd known her forever, and I hoped our newfound friendship would last past the party, whether I came to hang out with these people again or not.

We moved out into the den, where there was space for the two of us on a couch against the far wall. There was a window there, and since the curtains were open, we could see the bonfire was in full swing. Tons of guys stood around it smoking cigarettes and drinking their various drinks, and I saw some of them had brought girls along to the party, which made me feel better.

Seeing I wasn't going for any of the beer, Brittany offered me a glass of her wine she kept in the fridge, and I accepted it gratefully. After another hour or so of listening to music, people taking turns picking what they played on the sound system, I looked up to find a cute guy standing with Carson and Mike. He had a Bud Light in his hand, and was wearing a plain white t-shirt, jeans, black Adidas sandals, and a backward white baseball cap. He had an infectious smile, which hardly ever left his face as he talked animatedly with his friends, and I couldn't help watching him as he laughed loudly after listening to something Mike was saying.

His laugh caused a small smile to form on my own face, and the expression felt strange. It seemed to be the first genuine smile I'd had in the past two weeks, all the others having been forced to placate anyone I was around.

He must've felt my eyes on him, because suddenly they were connecting with his. He smiled at me, lifted his beer to his lips, and then went back to his conversation.

"That's Aiden Lanmon," Brittany said in my ear, making me jump. She giggled and continued, "He lives next door. He's over here all the time because he hates his roommate. Actually, we all hate his roommate."

"What's wrong with his roommate?" I asked curiously.

"He's now slept with three girlfriends of deployed buddies. *Three*. One, you just don't do that. There's a fucking code. And two, he's not even cute. He just gets to them when they're weak and vulnerable, and gives them a shoulder to cry on before taking advantage of their loneliness. Douchebag." She shook her head.

"Sounds like a creep," I muttered, and she nodded.

"Anyways, Aiden is my boyfriend, Chris', best friend. He's single...actually, I've never even seen him with a girl except for the time that got him that scar on his nose. But I know he's not gay. He's too much of a flirt to be gay."

"He's cute." I shrugged.

"I guess. I don't see him that way. He's like a brother to me. He does have pretty eyes though. I tell him all the time I wish I had his eyes. They're this cool hazel color, like bright green and brown got swirled together," she told me, taking a sip from her wine glass.

As we saw Carson and Mike move to the hallway leading to Mike's room, Brittany called, "Hey, Aiden. Come here."

"What are you doing?" I asked her in a panicked whisper.

"You aren't with Carson, right?"

"No. Just acquaintances, but—"

"Aiden," she cut me off as he walked up to where we sat on the couch, "this is my friend Kayla. She just moved back home from Texas."

"Texas? My family is in San Antonio," he remarked, sticking out his hand for me to shake.

"My brothers live in Houston," I told him, placing my hand in his. He shook it gently, seeming to think he'd break me if he did it too hard.

Do I look that fragile? It wouldn't surprise me if I did. I hadn't been eating much lately, and I noticed my clothes didn't fit as tightly as I normally liked them. Which is not a good thing, since I'm already naturally super thin.

"What were you doing in Texas?" he asked curiously.

Getting my heart broken and my soul crushed.

"I was there for a semester of school. My brothers thought I should see what it was like to live in a big city after living here all my life," I replied.

"You're actually from here? Weird," he stated.

"Yeah, there's not many of us." I shrugged.

"You want to go outside to the bonfire?"

His question caught me off guard, being such an abrupt change of subject, and I didn't answer for a minute as I took a sip from my wine glass. Brittany looked over at me and replied for me, "Yes, she'd love to," and placed her hand on my lower back to push me forward out of my seated position with a grin.

I glared at her as I stood up in front of Aiden, and when I turned to face him, I looked into the most beautiful hazel eyes I'd ever seen. She was right; they were incredible. He took my hand to guide me through the throng of people crowding the house, and when I looked back at Brittany, she gave me a wicked smile and wiggled her fingers at me.

We made our way out the back door and down more creaky wooden steps, then across the sparse, rutted grass until we reached the barrel blazing with a smoking fire.

"The good thing about living out here in the sticks is we get to burn shit whenever we want," Aiden remarked.

"Are y'all a bunch of pyros or something?" I asked lightly.

"What dude isn't?" He laughed. I looked up at him and noticed the scar Brittany had mentioned. It was a small black line that ran straight across the top of the bridge of his nose. He must've been able to tell where my eyes had landed, because he tapped the scar with a finger of his free hand not holding his beer bottle and said, "Yep, the dangers of being a pyro."

"What happened?"

"You're going to think I'm a dick," he warned.

"What dude isn't?" I threw his words back at him, and he chuckled.

"True. Okay, so I brought a girl to one of these parties, and ended up hitting it off with someone else. Well, turns out the girl I had brought told one of her guy friends what had happened, and we got into a fight by the bonfire. Our scuffle ended with me face planting into the fire," he explained.

"Wow, you are a dick," I joked.

"Yeah, well, ended up not going home with either of the girls because I had to go to the hospital and get my nose sewed up. They didn't clean it up good enough, because, ya know, military hospital, and it scarred with soot still in it. Now it looks like I got a fucking tattoo across my nose," he complained.

"Aw, that's okay. Gives you character," I assured him with another genuine smile.

We continued our conversation, topics coming easily as we talked about everything from where he was from to what I was studying in school. And at one point during the night, he ended up taking his shirt off, the bonfire mixing with the heat of the summer making several of the guys do the same. He was well-built and had a couple of tattoos, but it wasn't until he turned toward the house to go refill my wine glass that I saw the tattoo running across the top of his back. I don't know how long I stood there, nearly hyperventilating with an oncoming panic attack, when Brittany nudged me out of my stupor.

"You okay?" she asked, concerned.

"His tattoo," was all I could say.

"What about it?"

"He…he has his last name tattooed across his back."

CHAPTER Two

Gotta get out now, gotta run from this

I've always had a type. I've always been attracted to men with dark features and tattoos. It's just what gets my juices flowing I guess. There's been a long line of hot guys with dark hair, dark eyes, and lots of ink, but only one consumes my mind and plagues my dreams.

Jason.

He told me once that he got his last name tattooed across his upper back, because he was proud to be a Robichaux, even more driven to wear the name with honor because he was adopted.

At the time, I thought it was heartwarming. But as Aiden walked toward Brittany and me, carrying a Bud Light in one hand and a full glass of pink wine in the other, I found it haunting. I mean, of course the first dude who had gotten me out of my self-imposed shell and made me really smile and laugh in weeks just had to have the same tattoo as the man I really want, the one I would give anything to be with. He couldn't have a cool quote or a fucking butterfly tattooed there, could he? No.

When Aiden stepped up to us, he handed me the glass, and I accepted it with a quiet, "Thanks." Gone was the light, humorous mood from only minutes before, replaced with a dark thundercloud hanging directly over my head. After a few awkward moments of listening to Brittany and Aiden banter like siblings, she went back inside the house, leaving me alone with him once again.

"You all right?" he asked quietly.

"Yeah, I'm fine," I lied.

"Nah, something's wrong. You want to get away from all this craziness? I live right next door. We could watch a movie or something," he suggested.

My knees buckled as images of watching movies in Jason's bedroom flashed through my mind. Him making furious love to me while DVDs would play in the background, drowning out the cries he pulled from deep within me as he thrust into me, marking me as his.

"Whoa there," Aiden said, grabbing onto my arm. "I think you may have had a little bit too much to drink. Let's go chill out at my place for a little while." He looped my arm through his and walked me across the yard toward another white doublewide. I wanted so much to tell him no, that I just wanted to go home so I could cry myself to sleep again, but the pain in my chest was so overwhelming I just let him guide me, hoping getting away from the crowd of people would help me clear my head of the demons that just wouldn't leave me the fuck alone.

We made our way up a set of steps that looked like they were just built, the wood still bright and clean, not weathered in the slightest. He held the screen-door open for me, and he followed me inside. Upon entering his living room, the first thing I saw directly in front of me was a green felt-covered table, and another wave of horrified astonishment hit me.

You have got to be fucking kidding me.

In the center of the long oval table, its edges wrapped in black padded leather, sat a set of red, blue, green, and white clay chips, along with a deck of cards and a dealer chip.

Four of a kind.

Dark chocolate eyes looking up at me with amazed pride.

The smirk on those deliciously pouty lips.

"Do you play?" Aiden's question brought me out of the memory, and I looked up at him blankly.

"A little," I replied quietly.

"You look like you need to sit down before you fall down. Why don't you take a seat on the couch while I get you a bottle of water?" he suggested, nodding toward the sectional on the other side of the living room. I agreed and went to sit in the corner where the two halves met, the huge pillows lining the back of the suede couch engulfing me, comforting like a hug.

He came back and sat beside me, handing me an opened bottle of water. I took a sip as not to be rude, since I knew he'd probably never met a person who despised water as much as I do.

"Better?" he asked, pulling out a pack of cigarettes from his jeans pocket. I noticed they were Marlboros, but thankfully not the all too familiar red box. It was a golden color, something about a special blend. He pulled a dinner tray with an ashtray on it closer to him from the side of the couch and sat his beer down before lighting up. After the last ten minutes, I could definitely use one too, so following his lead, I pulled my own pack of menthols out of my crossbody bag and lit my own. It felt weird smoking inside someone's house, but I was happy to relax a little, enjoying the quiet.

"Better now," I finally replied, blowing out a long stream of smoke.

"So what brought you to the party?"

"I came with Carson." At his questioning look, I explained, "We're just acquaintances. I met him on MySpace, and he asked if I wanted to come so I could meet some new people. I haven't really done much since I got back home."

"So what do you like to do? If you haven't done much, then what would you like to be doing?"

Playing pool at Legends...cuddling up and watching Boondock Saints *with the man I love...drinking wine and smoking on a humid but comfortable back patio...*

"I like playing pool. I learned to play while I was in Texas, so I don't really know anywhere to play here. None of my friends play, so I don't have anyone to go with," is what I said aloud.

"Well, you're in luck. I just so happen to be badass at pool. I go all the time to a bar up the road. I'll take you sometime...if you want," he suggested.

Of course he plays pool. Why wouldn't he? Last name tattooed across his back, poker table in his house, self-proclaimed badass at pool...I swear to God, if he wears Realm, I'm going to flip shit. I took an inconspicuous sniff in his direction, but all I could smell was cigarette smoke and beer.

Maybe I was looking at this in the wrong light. Yes, it was really unnerving how many things were popping up that were so much like Jason, but instead of me running from it, what if it was a sign? These were all things I loved about him, and this nice guy, Aiden, had the same hobbies Jason did. And I just happened to find him only nine days after coming home from Texas? Maybe I was meant to meet Aiden.

What were the odds of meeting a man so much like the one I thought I was supposed to be with, at a random party where I knew absolutely no one? In a house full of strangers, he was the one who had caught my attention. He was the one who had whisked me away from the overwhelming crowd, rescued me.

Just like Jason always rescued me.

"Hey, where did you go?" Aiden asked, tilting my chin up to look into my eyes.

Wow, they really were the coolest eyes I'd ever seen. They weren't the dark chocolate eyes that made my heart skip a beat, but were beautiful, somehow comforting, and I took it as a good thing that at least one trait was solely Aiden's.

"Sorry, I just really miss the friends I made in Houston. We got very...close, and I'm still not used to being back home. I left for a reason, but now...here I am." I sighed.

"Yeah, it sucks making good friends and then having to leave them. I have to do that a lot, being in the Air Force. Not only when we move bases, but even on small trips and deployments. But hey, you can always talk to them on the phone, text, and computer shit, right? I don't have one of those profile things, but I heard you can find all sorts of long lost friends on there."

Talk to him on the phone? No. He never wants to speak to me again.

Text? No. His parents took texting off his phone, because he ran up the bill hundreds of dollars.

Computer shit? No. God, no. It would kill me to see him moving on with his life, seeing pictures of him.

"That's a good idea." I gave him a small smile and looked away to put out my cigarette in the ashtray. "Can I use your restroom?" I asked, standing and straightening out my top.

"Sure, it's just through there, first door on the left." He pointed to the opening in the wall he had gone through when he got my water.

"Thanks," I said, and hurried away to find a moment of solace.

When I was in the first grade, my mom threw me my first big birthday party, inviting everyone in my class at school along with the usual cousins and other family members. I can remember being so excited about the prospect of the party, but as everyone started showing up one by one, the crowd growing larger and larger, me being the center of everyone's attention, that excitement turned into anxiety.

I disappeared for a little while, and when my mom finally found me, I was hiding in the gazebo in my backyard. She loves telling the story about how when she discovered my hiding spot and asked why I was in there, I told her, "I just needed to get by myself, Mommy."

Right now, that's exactly what I was feeling. I just needed to get by myself. And Aiden's bathroom was the safest bet for a hiding spot without looking like a complete lunatic, which was another facet of emotion I was feeling at the moment.

Closing and locking the door behind me, I don't even turn on the light because there is a three-wick candle that's lit on the lid of the toilet, which actually does wonders as a sense of relief. I grasp the edge of the bathroom counter as I braced myself to catch my breath.

Just needed to get by myself.

No, you don't need to be by yourself. You need someone to take away the pain, because you sure as hell can't do it yourself.

I looked up into my reflection, focusing in on how the dancing flames of the candle made my eyes look wild, almost spooky.

The last time you were around candles, Jason had you at the side of his bed, fucking you from behind while you held onto his sheets for dear life.

The memory made me double over in pain, like I'd been punched right in the gut, and I rested my forehead on the back of my now stacked hands.

Yeah, you were bent over, just like that.

I took a deep breath and closed my eyes, wishing the thoughts away.

Wish in one hand and shit in the other, and see which one fills up faster. Don't wish the thoughts away; just fuck them away. After all, that's all you're good for, right? And once this one is done with you, you can just find anoth—

"Stop!" I shout, jerking myself upright. The evil little voice in my head, which just so happens to have a deep, Texan drawl, has been talking to me for the past nine days since I left Houston. It's the reason I dragged myself out of bed every morning, using the little inner strength I have left to defy what it tells me.

Hoping Aiden didn't hear my outburst, I turn on the faucet and rinse my face off with cool water. When I straighten and dry off on the towel hanging on the rack behind me, I gather myself enough to be in the presence of another human being and walk out to the living room.

"I'm feeling a lot better now. Thank you. I think I'm going to go find Carson to see if he'll take me back to my car. I rode with him from Pope."

"That's all right. I'll take you," Aiden offered, putting out his own cigarette before standing.

"You don't have to do that. You've done enough already."

"I really don't mind. Plus, he's probably already too wasted to drive you. Dude can't pace himself to save his life," he remarked, looking around, I assumed for his keys. "You ready?"

"Um...yes. Yes, thanks, Aiden. You're too sweet." I walked over to where he was holding the door open for me and made my way down the steps. I waited for him to lock his house up before following him to a white Pontiac Grand Am. He clicked the remote to unlock his doors, and I hopped into the passenger seat.

As we were pulling away, I regretted not exchanging numbers with Brittany. I really liked her, and hoped I'd get a chance to hang out with her again. And as we drove down the long, empty road back to Pope AFB, I thought that might definitely be in my future if Aiden had anything to do with it. He pressed and pressed until I finally agreed to go play pool with him tomorrow, and at my request, he promised he'd ask Brittany if she'd like to come.

Going through the security gate on the base, I handed over my driver's license for them to check, not having to get the car searched since Aiden is active duty and has the security sticker attached to his windshield. Soon, we pulled up next to my blue Malibu after I pointed it out to him in the dorm parking lot.

"Okay, so tomorrow. Eight o'clock at Little Reno. Let me get your number, and I'll call you from my phone so you can have it just in case you get lost or something," he said.

"Smooth," I chuckled, and then typed my cell number into his contacts. I handed it back to him, and then turned toward the door to get out, but he grabbed my arm.

"Hey, it was really great meeting you, Kayla. Don't worry. We'll show you how much fun it can be being back here in Fayettenam, and you'll forget all about those friends in Texas," he assured me.

I really hope so, I thought, and then I said it aloud.

He gave me one last infectious smile before letting my arm go with a gentle pat, and I opened the door to leave. As I opened my driver's side door, I looked over at him when he rolled down his window, and he called out, "Drive safe," before pulling away.

CHAPTER Three

Throw 'em back 'til I lose count

After I got home last night, I lay in bed for a while, thinking of all the crazy coincidences between Aiden and Jason. *Thinking? More like obsessing.* But my last thought before I finally fell asleep was that I'd just see where things went. I had only just met the dude. He could end up being someone to spend time with, who I become really good friends with, or I could never see him again after this weekend. Or, maybe it could grow into something more. For some reason, the similarities didn't feel like just a coincidence. Or I could be so freakin' desperate that I'm trying to give meaning to something completely insignificant. Either way, I'll let it play out.

So now here I sit in Anni's living room, my eyes

burning because the fumes of her hair dye are so strong as she sits next to me with her soggy mane piled into a clear shower cap. She's going dark this time, but I know she'll get tired of it in a couple of weeks and change it again.

I thought about letting her do mine—she's gotten really good at it, since she's had tons of practice—but I'm just not ready for such a change. All I can think of is Jason running his fingers through my long, dark brown locks, telling me how he'd never seen such shiny, beautiful hair before, that he could almost see his reflection in it. Or how he'd tangle it in his fist at the back of my head and pull me to him for one of his amazing, heart-stopping kisses. I know it might be a smart thing to change it up, but I just can't. Not yet, at least.

I told Anni all about last night, about Aiden and the similarities between him and Jason, and she's going with me tonight to the pool hall. She says she wants to see these 'mad pool skills' I learned in Texas, but I know she's going more to look after me. She has the same mixed feelings I do about him. It could be a good thing to use him to get past Jason. 'Use' has such a terrible implication. I don't want to *use* the poor guy, but I don't know any other word to describe having him around as a tool to move forward. I'm aware it's probably not the best thing in the world for my mental health to jump from one guy to the next, but how the hell else am I supposed to distract myself from the paralyzing pain I feel any time I allow myself to sit still?

And maybe it wouldn't even be like that. Maybe I could have genuine feelings for him. I mean, he did stand out to me last night in the crowd. I noticed him before he ever saw me. It was his smile and laughter that caught my attention before I even knew about his tattoo, or that he liked poker and pool. I was definitely attracted to him. Sure, it wasn't the overwhelming magnetic pull that I felt toward Jason, but at least something inside me could still feel attraction to someone else.

"We've still got a few hours before we need to head out. Do you want to watch a movie?" Anni asks as she puts the final touches of polish on her toenails.

"Yeah, sure. What do you want me to put in?" I stand up and make my way over to her drawer of DVDs.

"Put in that one with Johnny Depp and the horseless headman," she says, and I look over at her with my eyebrow raised. She has no idea what just came out of her mouth.

"Um...you mean the headless horseman?" I snort.

"Shut up, you know what I mean." She pouts.

It never gets old. The woman has dyslexia of the mouth, always saying shit backwards. I've missed spending so much time with her. She never fails to entertain me. I find *Sleepy Hollow*, put the DVD into the player, and walk over to her kitchen to grab the wine bottle I brought with me out of her fridge. I don't bother with a glass. I plop myself onto her couch, snickering as she growls when I make her hand holding the nail polish brush streak a line down the center of her big toe.

"Bitch, hand me that remover and a cotton ball. You're lucky I don't make you lick it off," she gripes.

"Gross." I hand over the bottle of pink liquid then twist

the top off the wine and take a swig directly from the bottle. When she looks at me with a peaked brow, I tell her, "Just getting started here so I don't have to spend so much at the bar."

"Uh-huh. Do you plan on finishing the whole thing before we leave? You know I have a cabinet full of wine glasses you left over here before you moved."

"You kept all of them?" I ask, trying to take the attention off the fact I did plan on polishing off the bottle, therefore not wanting to dirty up a glass.

"Wishful thinking that you'd be back," she says, and then looks at me with an apology in her green eyes.

"Don't worry about it, woman. The plan was always for me to go just for the semester. I never intended to stay longer, didn't even think about it until..." I choke up, not able to finish the thought.

She puts down the cotton ball and wraps her arms around me. I take a deep breath of her familiar, comforting scent, my soul being soothed just a little by the ever-present Elizabeth Arden perfume she's worn since the day I met her.

"It's okay," I sigh. I loosen my grip on her, and she lets go of me, and we both turn our attention to the movie.

By the time it's over, I need to start getting ready for the evening activities. We used to do this all the time. I'd bring over my clothes and makeup to get ready with Anni before going out to the club for a night of dancing. Unfortunately, the one club we used to go to is now overrun with drugs and prostitution, but we made plans to try out a different one next week. South Beach is a hip-hop club hooked onto a country bar called the Palomino. We had been to it once before, but at the time preferred Kagney's because of the male revue they had for two hours before they cleared the stage and started playing the dance music. It was sad to think we wouldn't be returning to the club we'd gone to nearly every weekend for two years before I left for Houston.

I grab my bag from beside her front door and head to her room at the back of her apartment. Changing from my comfy sweatpants and t-shirt into a tight pair of jean shorts and a hot pink tank top, I look into her full-length mirror as she walks in.

"What is this sorcery?!" she asks, astonished. "Is that leg skin I see?"

I chuckle lightly and reply, "Your eyes do not deceive you. My legs are, in fact, bare to the eyes of other life forms." Before, I would have never worn anything but jeans or pants, always self-conscious of my skinny legs. I guess one good thing I had taken from my relationship with Jason—if you could call it that—was that he'd made me feel beautiful, confident in the way I looked. He'd helped wash away most of the damage girls from my adolescent and teenaged years had done to the way I viewed myself.

I grab her lotion off her dresser and rub some into my legs. Then I walk up to the mirror and plop down in front of it cross-legged with my makeup bag in my lap. I see in the reflection as Anni walks into her en suite and turns on her curling iron, saying, "Well, hot damn. We'll have to go shopping for more stuff, so you can show off those sticks. Maybe go before Wednesday so we can find something new for South Beach."

"Sure. I have nothing else to do." I wasn't signing up for a summer semester at my community college. I had half a mind not to sign up for the coming fall either. I don't feel much like doing anything with my life at the moment, but I decide to save that thought for processing at another time. Tonight is all about having fun with my best friend, getting to know Aiden, and hopefully hanging out with Brittany if she comes. Oh, and getting wasted. That is definitely a must. I'm already halfway there after finishing the bottle of wine before the movie had even ended.

My face looks a little flushed in the mirror as I start applying my makeup, so I go light on the blush and focus more on my eyes. When I'm done, it looks on the outside like there's life in this empty vessel, and I practice a smile. Good to go.

I stand up, walk into Anni's bathroom, and sit on her toilet lid, watching as she makes quick work of curling her now dry locks. A short while into *Sleepy Hollow*, she had taken a shower to rinse out the hair dye and blew it dry to make sure the color was even. Perfect as always, she had strutted her way back into the living room, flipping her hair over one shoulder and then the other before turning around and g peeking at me over her shoulder like in a Clairol commercial. The girl looks good with any hair color, but I think this is my favorite. The super dark brown, almost black makes her green eyes pop like crazy.

I've always loved watching people get ready, whether it was my sister-in-law, Renee, when I was little, other girls getting their makeup and hair done before pageants, or even my granny, when she would take me to the beauty shop with her. For all the watching I've done though, I haven't learned a thing. Best I can do is blow dry mine straight. Sometimes I get fancy, and bobby pin a little poof back with the front of my hair, but it always ends up lopsided. So mine is just down tonight, as always when I go out. It's kind of like my security blanket, giving me just a little something to hide behind.

Anni isn't big on makeup. Her skin is flawless, and she has the most adorable freckles, so she only applies a little mascara, and some gloss to her lips. She always complains she hates her lips, because she says they are too thin. I personally think it just makes the attention fall more on her gorgeous green eyes.

When she's all done, we make our way back into her bedroom, which has clothes piled on every surface, and shoes stacked in every nook and cranny of available space. I can't count how many times I've helped her organize all her stuff, but somehow, only a few days later, you practically have to swim through her room.

She looks at me and ponders aloud, "Hmmm, if you're wearing that, I think I'll wear my new shorts. But no pink. You know I don't do pink. That's your thing."

"Not even on Wednesdays," I sing from her closet as I slide hanger after hanger holding shirts and dresses from one side to the other, looking for a top to go with the jean shorts she's holding up for me to see.

"You and that dumb movie. You're still not over it? It's been what, a year since it came out?"

I look over my shoulder at her and say haughtily, "You can't sit with us."

"Who, you and the voices in your head? Find me a top, bitch." She jerks her head toward her closet.

Before I turn back to the task though, I stage-whisper to her, "Horseless headman," then laugh and duck when she chucks her shorts at my head.

We finally decide on a low-cut white shirt for her to wear, and when she puts on the outfit, the next challenge is finding a pair of shoes. She has about a trillion, and almost all of them are cute and would go with the outfit she's wearing; the problem is finding a match. Every time we think we find a set, one of the shoes has disappeared from the last place we saw it. Eventually, we unearth a pair of espadrilles that make her legs look a mile long. She'd been a horseback rider all her life, so her legs are much different than mine. Where mine are long and skinny, hers are thick with defined muscle.

"Bitch," I tease for making me move fast while wine is in my system, and I smack her on her non-existent ass. At least I have her beat there.

Feeling my buzz heighten after a nicotine break out on Anni's balcony, it's finally time to leave. Neither of us has ever been to the pool hall we are meeting Aiden at, and as if he can sense we are heading to him, I receive a text message.

Aiden: About to leave my place. See you soon. Britt coming too.

I smile down at my phone. I'm not sure whether the expression was brought on by him texting me or from the happy news that Brittany will be coming too, but I don't question it. I let the little bit of excitement I feel carry me out to Anni's red Mustang, where we blast music and sing along with the radio as I shout directions out to her that I had printed off my computer before I left my house.

About thirty minutes later, we pull into the small parking lot of Little Reno. It doesn't look like much, just a generic one-story building with blacked out windows, and a brightly lit sign with the bar's name. As Anni and I enter, there's a closet-size room with a window, with a weathered looking biker-esque woman checking IDs sitting on a stool. We show her our licenses, and she marks my hands with black Xs, but not Anni's, since she turned twenty-one last August.

Walking into the main bar area, it looks just like any other, with round tables and lots of chairs scattered throughout, neon beer brand signs glowing along the perimeter of the ceiling. In the center is a rectangular bar with stools surrounding it, and off to the right is a small dance floor with a disco ball spinning above it. Looking farther to the right, there are a couple of stairs leading up to an entirely different room full of pool tables, which we can see through the giant window on the opposite side of the dance floor.

We hear the bell above the entrance ring, and after a few seconds, in walks Brittany, looking just as cute as she did yesterday, in a pastel yellow tank top and jeans with a white belt. Behind her, Aiden walks in, not looking up as he puts his ID back in his wallet, barely missing running into Brittany.

"Hey! I'm so glad you had him invite me. I was

bummed when I went back outside and couldn't find you last night," she tells me, giving me a quick hug.

"Brittany, this is my best friend Anni. And Anni, this is Aiden." I gesture to him as he holds his hand out to shake hers.

She looks at him suspiciously for a moment, probably doing her usual guy-assessment, before finally placing her hand in his for a solid shake. There's nothing prissy about my bestie. I can't help but grin when Aiden flexes his hand a little when they let go.

"So do y'all want to get a drink before we get a table?" he asks. I hold up my Xed hands and stick out my bottom lip. "Don't worry about that. I don't turn twenty-one 'til December, but I know the owners. If you're with me, they won't say shit."

I look at Anni, who is frowning at him, so I nudge her lightly with my elbow. She's always so protective of me, hating it when I break rules. When we used to go clubbing, she was always a mother bear, never letting me accept drinks from guys, even when we saw them take it directly from the bartender and placed it in my hands. I could only drink it if the bartender handed it me, which was kind of hard when I wasn't of age. That's why we liked to go to Kagney's, because we'd just wash the Xs off. A lot of the other places around here, it was the opposite. You had to have a wristband or a stamp in order to drink.

"I'll take a glass of white ziff if they have it, thanks," I tell him. Anni opens her mouth to refuse, but I send a glare her way that stops her in her tracks.

"I'll take a Jack and Coke," Brittany requests, and when Aiden looks over to Anni, she just shakes her head. If I'm drinking, she won't even take a sip. Girl takes her job as a DD very seriously. The only time she ever really drinks is when we are at her place, and even then, the occasions are very few and far between.

When Aiden returns with our drinks, I'm surprised when he doesn't go back to the bar to get a set of pool balls. All the places we went to play in Texas, you got your set and then went and picked your table. Instead, we follow him directly to the back of the room, where he pulls out a couple rolls of quarters from his pocket and sits them at the small table next to the pool table. He unrolls several quarters and walks over to the wooden edge of the green felt-covered surface. There is a plastic holder with the numbers one through seven printed in circular slots, and I watch as Aiden takes the coins and fills up the circles.

He looks up to see my confused face, and explains, "You put the quarters in the slots to show you're claiming the table for that many games. As long as you keep the slots filled, no one will jack your shit."

At that moment, I hear Aiden's name being called as a large group of guys I recognize from last night walks up the couple of stairs and into the billiard room. Each one does the guy handshake-hug thing they all seem to do, and after a few moments of them discussing whether they want pitchers of beer or other drinks, the huddle disperses. Some of the guys go back down the stairs to the bar there, and a few of them go to the bar that's against the back wall of the room we're in.

They gradually return, and I'm kind of pissed when instead of offering me a pool cue, Aiden hands it to one of his buddies. After all, wasn't it he who invited me to come play, since it was the one thing I told him I enjoyed doing? I sit down in the chair across from Anni, take a sip of my wine, and then reach into my bag to pull out my cigarettes, lighting one and pulling the ashtray in the center of the table closer to me. When I look up at her, she's watching me intently, and I can tell she knows I'm upset.

Oh shit...

I know the moment the idea clicks into her vindictive little mind. My eyes widen, and I whisper-hiss, "Don't you dare, Anni Lee. We just met these people. Don't embarrass me."

"He had us drive all the way out here for you to get to know him, and then his stupid friends show up and he doesn't even introduce you. And now, after inviting you out to play, you're over here sitting and getting sloshed, while his buddies take over the pool table. What the ever-loving fuck?" She abruptly stands, and I grab her hand as she walks toward Aiden, where he is focusing on the shot he is about to take, but she shakes me off. I watch, horrified, as she makes her way over to him, and just as he's about to take his shot, she hits the back of his stick, sending the cue ball flying across the table.

He stands up straight and turns, a half-smiling, half-pissed look on his face, obviously thinking it was one of his friends playing a joke on him. The look of surprise is almost laughable when he sees it's my very short-tempered, fuming best friend. "Uh—"

"Shut it," she cuts him off. "What is the deal with you bringing my girl out here to play, and these assholes show up, and suddenly she doesn't exist? Do you think that's the polite thing to do when you're supposed to be getting to know a chick?"

"Uh—"

"Did I say you could talk? No," she states, and he looks confused.

"You just ask—"

"I wasn't done. You can speak whenever I'm finished asking you all my questions. My best friend just had to crawl her sweet ass back to this shithole of a town, and she had actual hope today when she was telling me about this 'nice guy' she met last night who actually seemed to want to take her out for a good time. Does she look like she's having any goddamn fun?"

I just know she gestures toward me, where I'm now slouched down in my chair with my glass of wine cradled to my chest, my head thrown back, looking up at the ceiling in mortification, my cigarette sticking out the corner of my mouth, because I can feel everyone's eyes on me. I probably look like a train wreck, smoke and all.

"Well…are you going to answer me?"

I can't help but snort at Anni's question. The poor boy she's giving hell probably has no idea what just hit him. I almost feel bad for him…almost.

"I didn't know my friends were coming. I'm sorry I got distracted," he tells her, and then I watch as he moves toward me. He kneels down next to me and puts his warm hand on my bare thigh, sending a shiver up my leg. "I'm sorry I kind of left you. My buddy and I have a bet going from a game left over from last week, and that got in my head and pushed everything else out. If you want, I can tell them to open their own table, and then you and I can play on this one," he says quietly enough only I can hear.

"That's okay. I'll just wait my turn." I take a sip of my wine, tapping my cigarette out in the ashtray.

He leans forward and whispers, "Your friend is scary."

"That was nothing," I warn, looking him in the eye.

He sucks air in through his teeth before standing up again, then bends at the waist to say in my ear, "Then I better be a good boy."

I feel the corners of my lips lift, and I shift in my seat just as Anni lowers herself haughtily into her seat. When he goes back to the game, she raises a perfectly tweezed brow and sasses, "That shade of pink in your cheeks looks good on you. I should embarrass you more often."

"Oh, you do it quite enough, thanks. Bitch," I hiss, finishing off the wine in my glass.

Just as I'm about to set the empty glass on the table, it's lifted from my hand from over my head, and I turn to see Aiden's retreating back as he heads to the bar.

"My work here is done," Anni brags.

The rest of the night is spent taking turns playing pool, Anni, Brittany, and me dancing on the tiny dance floor whenever a line dance or a hip-hop song comes on, and drinking...lots and lots and *lots* of drinking. The more I drink, the less and less I think about eyes the color of Hershey Kisses, pillow-soft lips, and tattooed arms made of steel attached to a body that was made for nothing but pleasure.

My focus turns to not falling, and trying not to pee on myself from laughing so hard at Aiden and Anni, who have now grown accustomed to each other and have decided it's enjoyable to try to destroy each other's ego. Their banter was making me uncomfortable at first, but after they both had reassured me it was all in good fun, and with a healthy dose of sweet pink wine, I found their bashing hilarious. I played exactly two games of pool before I couldn't bend over the table without toppling over, and darts were abruptly taken out of my hands by a smiling Aiden, who was growing cuter and cuter as the night went on.

Before Anni has to practically carry me out to her car, I hug every single one of the guys, and Brittany, telling them each that I love them, and even kiss Aiden on the cheek. He tries to do that thing where the guy turns his head to make the kiss land on his lips, but I catch my momentum just in time, grab his face between my hands, and hold him still to smack my lips against his cheekbone. He gives me his infectious smile one last time, before I fall into the Mustang's passenger seat, and before he closes the door behind me, I slur something about him coming to shake his ass with us on Wednesday. I'm pretty sure he agrees, and after the door is shut, I see Brittany mouth, *'I'll be there!'* through my window.

I slightly come to as Anni helps me up her stairs to her apartment. I'm vaguely aware of fighting with her, wanting a cigarette out on her balcony. I win, and she sits right next to me, like she thinks I'm going to throw myself over the iron railing. And then I'm in her bed in my t-shirt and undies. She won't leave me the whole night, because she thinks I might get sick in my sleep and not wake up.

I love my best friend, is my last thought before I sink into a black oblivion.

Chapter Four

Kayla's Chick Rant & Book Blog
June 3, 2005

Wednesday night was...interesting. South Beach has changed a lot since the last time I was there. It's actually pretty cool how it's set up. One side of the club has all black walls with blacklights lining the ceilings and bars, and beach scenes glow on each wall. There is a massive dance floor, with a stage and poles where brave—or in my case, completely trashed—club goers can show off their moves as the thumping bass of the hip-hop music blares through the huge speaker systems on each side of the floor.

On one of the walls is a giant open doorway, and walking through it is like being teleported into a completely different universe. One second you are in the raging party atmosphere of South Beach, and the next, you are in the relaxed and happy-go-lucky ambiance of the Palomino Club. There is a large, circular wooden dance floor in the middle of the room, with steps in the center leading down into a small area with a few tables and chairs. A railing lines the interior, presumably so dancers don't fall into the hole as they are spinning in their cowboy boots while two-stepping.

There is a bar on either side of the saloon-inspired club, but what caught my attention were the two mirror-covered saddles rotating over the dance floor in place of the normal disco balls.

Anni and I participated in every line dance that was played, from "Stars On the Water," to "Copperhead Road," to my new favorite, "Strokin'." Aiden even joined in for the "Cotton-eyed Joe." Brittany...let me tell ya...that girl's got some moves! I could easily see her in a hip-hop music video.

I drank the night away, Aiden teaching me a trick of buying just a coke or juice, and then—with his fake ID—he'd buy a round of shots and just pour one in my cup. Easy peasy. Anni must've been getting used to the fact I'm basically trying to numb myself, accepting it's the only way I can function without wanting to break down every five minutes. She didn't say anything about the amount I was drinking, didn't try to hinder me in any way, but still, she never left my side. She'd allow it, but she'd watch over me while it happened. So I felt secure enough to just give in to the liquor and the blaring music, letting the beat fill the emptiness I felt inside.

I laughed often, Aiden impressing me with his dance skills, and I even slow danced with him a few times. There were no fireworks, or even a spark, but what I did feel was safe, taken care of while I was in his arms. And I think that's what I really need right now. I don't know if I'll ever feel the magic I felt with Jason, but at least I now know I can feel comfortable being held by another guy.

We exchanged email addresses over texts, so for the past couple of days, we've been writing back and forth to each other non-stop. He doesn't have a MySpace, but I copy and paste the cute 'about me' questionnaire posts that make their way around the site, fill out all my answers, and then send them to him. About an hour later, I'll get a response with all his answers, and I find myself smiling as I read them.

I now know all his favorite foods, places to go, all about his childhood, his worst fears, and his embarrassing moments. All within a week, I feel like I really know this guy. Anni thinks I'm rushing things, that I'm getting attached too quickly, and maybe I am, but I'm...I'm desperate. I'm desperate to heal this gaping wound I feel in my soul. And when I'm talking to Aiden, and hanging out with him, it's still there, but it's a little bit more bearable.

So I'm going to latch on to that tiny bit of ease I get when I'm around him, and I'm going to use it as a lifeline, because God knows what would happen to me if I didn't at least have that.

Help me, I'm holding on for dear life

A week later

It's party night at Brittany's house, as usual. She and I have been getting really close over MySpace and texting. She's happy to have a girl to talk to while her boyfriend is deployed, and I like how free-spirited she is. She's a goofball, and it's fun to mix her personality with Anni's mothering ways. Anni said she feels like she now has two daughters to look after.

Anni is driving us out to Spring Lake for the party. I've been letting her read all the emails between Aiden and me, and she's warmed up to him, seeing how much time he spends writing me throughout his work day, when he should be fixing C-130s. He's an airplane mechanic, which is kinda hot. He looks very impressive in his camouflaged BDUs, always with a little bit of black grease smeared somewhere on his face.

The first time I saw him like that, when we met for lunch one day right off base, I felt a little tremor of nausea when the image of the first time I met Jason, in his driveway when he was fixing his truck, immediately popped into my head. But in his usual way, Aiden cracked a joke about being a grease-monkey, and my attention was brought back to the present.

I've been to these parties for the last three weekends, and this is Anni's first time going since she usually has to work on Friday nights. I've warned her that the guys can get a little rowdy, but they are all good men, so she should be on her best behavior and lighten up while we're here. She promised she wouldn't pick any fights, and that's probably the most I can ask for.

I also informed her that I was going to stay here tonight. Aiden invited me to go to the beach for the weekend, and we'll be leaving first thing in the morning. She wasn't happy about that one bit, even inviting herself along, but I told her not this time. I wanted to see if I could handle being alone with another man without having her there as a security blanket. He's been doing a great job of bringing me out of my funk during our lunches, so there's hope.

I don't really get what he sees in me, why he bothers cheering me up, a girl he only met two weeks ago, who clearly has issues. I voiced this to Anni, and she said if she were someone who didn't know me, who didn't know I was normally an overly-bright, perky, almost annoyingly cheerful person, she'd just think I was a little shy. Apparently I'm good at hiding how desolate I feel.

I tell myself to stop questioning it and just go along for the ride, wherever this may lead me. I mean, I can't feel any worse than I already do, right? I'm pretty much at rock bottom. Things can only look up from here.

The house is already packed by the time we get there, so—bottle of wine in hand—we make our way out the back door to the bonfire. Aiden has saved me a fold-up camping chair next to him, and Brittany brings over two more for her and Anni. Next thing I know, I'm trying my first sake bomb. Dropping a shot glass full of Japanese sake into a Solo cup halfway full of beer, the three of us chug our drinks while Anni looks on in disgust. Surprisingly, it goes down pretty easy, and about an hour later, we do another...and another, until finally, I can't feel my face.

I'm vaguely aware of Anni arguing with Aiden about taking me home, but I drunkenly turn that down. I'm actually looking forward to this weekend at the beach. So I listen to her give him explicit instructions not to leave my side for a second during the night, and he agrees. Something is said about no funny business, and I hear the defense in his voice as he responds. I can't even stand up on my own, and my head flops back as Aiden lifts me into his arms, carrying me next door to his house. He carefully makes his way through the front door, around the corner, through the kitchen to the hallway, and then through what I assume is his bedroom door.

I'm confused as I'm laid on the bed, because the mattress feels weird. At the look on my face, he explains it's an air mattress, and the last thing I remember is asking him why he doesn't have a real bed.

CHAPTER Five

Sun is up, I'm a mess

Pain like I've never felt in my life explodes in my head the second my eyes open. I groan, turning onto my other side, pulling the covers over my face. I hear a deep chuckle next to me, and crack one eye open again to see Aiden smiling down at me, where he's propped up on his elbow.

The air mattress moves me higher as he shifts to grab something off the dinner tray next to him, and I see the alarm clock sitting on it reads 9:32am. He turns back to me and opens his hand to reveal two Tylenols, and when I take them, he grabs a bottle of water off the tray, opening it up and handing it to me. It actually hurts to swallow, and I squeeze my eyes closed as I gulp down the water.

"The fuck did I drink last night?" I ask in a scratchy whisper, remembering trying something other than my wine.

"Sake bombs," he tells me. "You took them like a champ, which is surprising. I thought you said you don't like beer."

"I don't," I groan, hiding my face in the pillow.

I feel his fingers start in the center of my forehead and gently slide their way across to my ear as he pushes my hair out of my face. I don't know how I feel about the would-be sweet gesture, but I don't have time to dwell on it, because suddenly his hand runs through the back of my hair, and he uses it to turn my face back up to his. He looks down at me with those swirling green and brown eyes, and I see real care in their depths. It makes me want to cry. I'm scared to believe the emotion, because the last time I thought a man cared about me, I ended up getting fucked. Literally.

The want to cry turns into an actual action, and his brow furrows as he sees my eyes tear up. "What's the matter? Did I hurt you?" he asks, loosening his grip in my hair.

My breath hitches and a single tear slides down the bridge of my nose. "Not yet."

His head pulls farther away so he can see me better, and I can almost hear the wheels spinning in his head. Is he thinking about if it's even worth getting involved with my fucked-upness? Is he wondering if I'm too damaged to deal with? Because I sure am. I'm wondering if I should let this guy get involved with me. He's so full of spirit, so happy and playful. Won't I just bring him down?

A few moments pass, and when I'm sure he's about to pull away and send me packing, he does the opposite. He leans closer, and in the most soothing and sweet tone, he whispers, "I don't know who or what hurt you, but if you let me, I'm going to kiss and make it better. Is that all right with you?"

I look into his eyes, wanting so much to believe he truly can make everything all better, so I nod once.

Nothing. Absolutely nothing. My heart doesn't speed up, lights don't go off behind my closed eyelids, butterflies don't set off inside my belly...nothing. The kiss is...nice. The actual physical touch of his lips against mine is pleasant, and I know if I wasn't dead inside, it would have been one of the better kisses I've had in my life. But still, it doesn't hold a candle to the last man I kissed, the man I know my soul cries out for as Aiden takes the kiss deeper, lightly running the tip of his tongue across the seam of my lips.

I pull back at the pain I feel in my heart and cover my mouth with my hand. He looks at me confused for a moment, but taking in my position, he chuckles and questions, "You worried about morning breath? Anni brought your bag in from her car before she left last night. You want me to grab your toothbrush for you?"

I force a smile behind my hand, hoping it reaches my eyes as I nod. I need him away from me for a minute. I need to get ahold of myself before I have a full-blown panic attack over Jason while lying in another man's bed.

He moves off the bed, making me bounce a little as the air mattress shifts. When he leaves the room, I tangle my fingers in the front of my shirt, pulling the neckline down because I feel like I can't breathe. Why am I freaking out so badly? On my drive home from Texas, I stopped in Florida and stayed overnight with an old friend-with-benefits. We'd drank his sister's wine on his humid back porch, listening to the sound of crickets chirping until we ended up falling into his bed for a night of straight fucking. We hadn't kissed, not bothering with the affection, just got right down to business.

It hadn't affected me the way this one little kiss with Aiden did. Was it because he'd been familiar, an old friend I'd done it with before? Was it because there wasn't anything emotional about the sex we had? Or was it because I had been going through the anger part of loss, trying to rid myself of the feelings Jason had given me?

What stage am I in now? I never went through the denial part, I don't think. Jason had made it perfectly clear he didn't want me anymore; there was no denying that. At the time, I'd thought, *Is this really happening?* But I was quick to realize it most certainly was. I must be going through the bargaining and depression stages, bargaining with myself, saying if I can just make myself feel something for Aiden, then the feelings for Jason will disappear.

If only I could make them go away.

If only there were a way to forget he even existed.

I look up as Aiden reenters the room and holds out my toothbrush like he found the winning prize. His grinning face lightens my panic to a dull ache, and I sit up carefully, not wanting to add to my pounding headache.

"Check-in time at the hotel isn't until three, and it only takes two and a half hours to get to Myrtle Beach, so you have plenty of time to get over your hangover before we need to leave. I'll make us some breakfast while you do your thing in the bathroom across the hall. I have a magical cure that'll fix you right up," he assures me, and as I go to take my toothbrush from him, he wraps his other arm around my waist and pulls me to him. He doesn't try anything, just holds me to him in a sweet embrace, and I draw strength from the hug. I breathe out a long sigh, and when he finally lets me go, I feel steadier on my feet.

He wasn't lying. Aiden's breakfast of scrambled eggs with melted cheese and buttered toast did the trick of settling my stomach, and mixed with the pain relievers, my head was back to its normal, albeit cloudy, state.

We'd left his house close to noon and arrived at our hotel in Myrtle Beach around three after stopping for lunch at Waffle House along the way. We've spent the past few hours just chilling on the beach, and I've enjoyed running my toes through the beautiful, soft white sand after only seeing the brown, seaweed-covered dirt in Galveston for my past couple of beach trips.

He uses his fake ID to buy beer and a few bottles of wine at the liquor store next to our hotel, and after eating a seafood dinner at one of the small joints off the strip, we go back to our hotel to drink on our balcony. The weather is perfect. I soak up the last rays of sun as it sinks into the horizon, my feet propped up on the railing as I slink down further into my chair, ashing my cigarette in the ashtray in the center of the glass table between us.

After a while of comfortable silence as he finishes off his third beer, replenishing my second glass of wine, he asks, "You know those questionnaire things you send me?"

"Yeah." I look at him suspiciously.

"What if we do something like that, only out loud? There's some stuff I'd like to ask you that weren't on one of the surveys." He gives me a wicked grin.

"You mean like 20 Questions?" I look down into my wine glass, fighting back the dread bubbling up and threatening to ruin the good day I've had since I brushed my teeth this morning.

"Yeah. I mean, you can always pass if you don't feel comfortable answering one," he assures me, sensing my shift in mood.

I sigh and then take a deep breath before agreeing with a nod.

"Okay, great...ummm. Well, shit. Now that I can ask, I'm drawing a blank," he confesses with a smile.

"I'll go first then," I offer, and he nods eagerly. "Tell me about your last girlfriend."

He huffs out a short laugh, and then answers, "Well, I would...but I've never had one."

My head jerks back and I feel my eyebrows pull together with astonishment. "Wait...what?"

"I mean, I've gone on more than one date with the same girl before, but I've never been in an actual serious relationship. Never found anyone I wanted to spend that much time with." He shrugs. "What about you?"

The abrupt turnaround in the conversation snaps me out of my disbelief, and pain sears from my stomach up to my heart. Feeling like I got sucker-punched, I chug the rest of my wine and light another cigarette. "That bad, huh?" he asks, standing to take my wine glass from me just inside the room through the sliding glass door, where the bottle sits in the mini fridge. He refills it to the top and hands it to me, sliding the door closed again.

"You have no idea. Thanks," I say, giving him a cheers against his Bud Light bottle.

"You don't have to answer. I'll ask something el—"

"No, that's okay," I interrupt. "It might be therapeutic." He gives me a gesture to continue, and I take another deep breath, trying to sort in my mind what exactly to say. I don't want to reveal too much. I don't want him to know just how much Jason meant to me, what he still means to me, but I would like him to know why I space out sometimes. At least twice a day, he pulls me out of my head with his gentle question of 'Where'd you go?'

"There was a guy in Texas I got really close to. He... he became important to me, like...he was my best friend. I developed feelings for him, but he didn't feel the same way. It's kind of stupid to be heartbroken over someone you weren't even in a real relationship with, right? But here I am. I'll get over it. It just sucked not having the feelings returned is all." I try to make light of what really happened, hoping he won't sense there was much, *much* more to the situation than what I was giving him, and I breathe a sigh of relief when he asks a different question, until I hear what the actual question is.

"When was the last time you had sex?"

"Wow, you move right to the juicy stuff, huh?" I ask, trying to stall while deciding if I'll tell him the truth, or feed him some bullshit to save face.

"That definitely wasn't on the questionnaire you sent me," he laughs.

I purse my lips together and narrow my eyes. "You first," I bargain.

He smirks at me, and then gives in. "About a month ago."

I wait for him to elaborate, but he's not forthcoming, so I prompt, "And..."

"Oh, you want details. Is that a good idea? I mean, you're not one of those girls who hunt down exes like a crazy stalker, are you?" he jokes.

"According to you, you don't have any exes," I

remind him.

"Touché. It was just some girl who came to one of the weekend parties. She was a friend of one of my buddies, and it was a one-time thing. Horrible. Would definitely never happen again."

"What was so horrible about it?" I ask curiously.

"We were both entirely too drunk...aaand I got a good look at her without my drunk goggles on the following weekend."

I scoff at that and call him a douche, and after he laughs, he reminds me it's my turn to answer the question. I never told him when exactly I got back home, so I flub the timing a little bit and answer, "Mine was also about a month ago. Friend with benefits on my drive home. Stopped in Florida to visit with him, got really drunk, and it just kind of happened." I hold my breath for his reaction, and exhale silently when he gives me a chin lift.

"Totally been there. Not Florida, but in Michigan. Went home to visit my dad on leave and ended up getting drunk with an old high school friend," he reveals.

With the wine flowing through my veins like a lazy river, I feel brave and ask what has been on my mind since we started spending so much time together. "You just said you've never had a real relationship because you hadn't met anyone you wanted to see that much. Well, we've been talking and hanging out nearly every day since we met two weeks ago, and here I am, spending the weekend with you in Myrtle Beach. Does that mean you might...maybe see this going somewhere?"

He looks out at the ocean for a moment, then reaches behind his head and rubs the back of his neck, looking nervous for the first time since I met him. I'm about to rebuke my question, when he finally stands, comes over to my side of the table, and then stoops down in front of me.

"That's actually why I invited you down here. I...it sounds corny, but I wanted to ask you if you'd like to be my girlfriend." He looks up at me with those beautiful hazel eyes, and I see a little bit of fear mixed with hope.

How long? How fucking long did I wait to hear that question come from the lips of the man my heart belongs to? How many times did I drive down to Friendswood from Kingwood thinking, *Today is the day!* wishing and praying it would finally be the day Jason would ask me to be his girl.

And now, after only two weeks, this sweet, handsome, likeable guy, who had never asked anyone to be his girlfriend before, readily offered me the question I longed to be asked for months upon months by another man. Was this some sort of sick joke God was playing on me? I can't help the little bit of anger I feel, mostly towards Jason. Why couldn't he have just loved me the way I loved him?

Or maybe this is where I was being led. Was I meant to end up back in North Carolina at that exact time, so I could meet Aiden? Either way, I take a deep breath and throw caution to the wind. Fuck it. Why not? It's not like the dust pile that was my heart could get any more broken. "I'd really like that," I tell him with a small smile, which grows bigger when he hollers a "WOOHOO!" over the balcony, turns back toward me, and then lunges up to kiss me.

It makes me sad that my natural reaction is to jerk away, but I force myself to lean into the kiss, fighting my flight instinct until it eventually goes away. The kiss still doesn't provoke any profound feeling within me, but it's a little more content than the one from this morning. I try to draw comfort from just the closeness of being wrapped in the arms of another human being, and it begins to work.

Focusing all of my attention on the physical act of what we are doing—lips pressed against mine, tongue delving into my mouth, calloused hands skimming up my arms, up my neck, and into my hair, a warm, muscular male body pressing up against the front of my much smaller frame—with the help of the wine now racing through my system, I'm able to push aside all emotion and zero in on my body's natural instincts, and give in to what Aiden wants.

CHAPTER Six

Maybe tomorrow it won't be this hard

The next morning, instead of waking up to pain in my head, I wake up sore all over. Being the first time having sex with Aiden, I was able to step outside myself and pretend not to have my usual hang-ups, like my self-consciousness and doubts in my sexual abilities. He had no idea what I was normally like in bed, so I let myself become a different person, one of the brave heroines in one of my books, who was self-assured and confident in herself.

I don't know if I was utterly shocked or completely expecting it, since it hadn't happened with my friend in Florida either, but just as before I met Jason, I wasn't able to reach my orgasm. God knows I tried, even moving us into positions that never failed when Jason and I would heatedly grind ourselves against each other with all-consuming passion. It just wouldn't happen.

I fought with myself in the moment, trying to decide whether to fake it like I used to or keep the promise I made myself never to do that again. In the end, it didn't matter. I don't think he could tell either way, because he was so engrossed in the pleasure he was feeling himself.

He was by no means a selfish lover. He made sure to lavish me with affectionate kisses and caresses, but it was like he was overwhelmed with what he was experiencing, while I still felt hollow inside, instincts eventually giving way to the realization I was desperately trying to fuck the memories out of my head once again.

After taking a quick shower together, we watched an action flick on TV. Aiden tried to hold me during the movie, and I let him for a few minutes, but then lightly complained I was hot and rolled over to my side of the bed. I lay there with my eyes closed feigning sleep for the longest time, even after hearing Aiden's quiet snoring, and even past another movie; I'm not even sure what it was, because all I saw on the backs of my eyelids was the handsome face of my lost love.

I obviously eventually lost consciousness, because now, as I sit up and look around, trying to get my bearings as I take in the tidy hotel room, I feel groggy and unrested. As far as I know, Aiden doesn't have any plans for us today. Checkout time is at 11:00am, and I read on the alarm clock beside our bed that it's a little past ten. When I get home this afternoon, I plan on sleeping through 'til tomorrow.

I nudge him on the shoulder and let him know what

time it is, and after a dramatic stretch and loud yawn, he looks up at me with a grin on his face. "We have enough time for another round before we leave," he suggests, waggling his eyebrows at me.

I fight the frown tickling the corners of my mouth and force a laugh. "You're insane. I'm too sore from last night's escapades," I tell him with as much sensuality as I can muster.

"You okay?" he asks, sliding himself closer and wrapping his arms around my waist, pressing a kiss to my side. It tickles and sends a shiver throughout my body. He takes it as a sign I might be warming up to the idea of another round after all, and begins sliding one of his hands lower. I swat it away and hop out of bed, wearing a T-shirt and undies, and quickly find my jean shorts to throw on.

There. Safe from roaming hands, and halting any thoughts of a quickie before we leave. I have to admit the small, probably unconscious pout on Aiden's face is kind of adorable, but it still doesn't change my mind about getting ready to leave. I'm ready to be home, where I can call Anni and tell her about yesterday.

After packing up our few belongings, we drop off the keycard at the front desk and make our way to his Grand Am. We talk every once in a while, but most of the trip back to Fayetteville is spent listening to music, taking turns choosing songs from his giant binder of CDs.

A couple of hours later, we pull into my parents' winding driveway. Like a gentleman, he hops out and comes around to my side to open my door, then moves to the trunk to get my bag out for me. When I reach to take it from him, he swings it behind his back and shakes his head, then nods toward my front door.

Oh, God. He wants to come inside?

I don't think I'm ready to introduce my new boyfriend to my family just yet—my dad is probably at the movies, his usual Sunday ritual after church—but Aiden's really giving me no choice. I don't want to be a bitch and tell him he can't come in. I internally sigh and head toward my front porch. We climb the couple of steps to the door, and I use my key to unlock the big, wooden door before giving it a hearty shove inward.

Aiden follows me in and whistles when he sees we've walked into our great room. There are a couple of couches and comfy chairs in a semi-circle around my baby grand piano, and on the wall above it is one of my old pageant portraits. He steps off the carpeted landing and down onto the hardwood floor, moving closer to look at the life-size picture of me in all my 90s, big hair glory, with my gold and rhinestone crown perched on top.

He turns back to me with a grin and boasts, "Damn, girl! You were smokin'!"

I snort a laugh and reply, "Thanks, Chester. I was only fifteen in that picture, you perv."

He scoffs and looks toward the picture again, exclaiming, "Fifteen?! Are you serious?"

I nod and start moving farther into my house, past the dining table, and the china hutch displaying all my crowns and sashes, and I can't help but chuckle when I hear Aiden's quiet, "Holy shit," as he catches sight of them.

"How many pageants have you won?" he asks as we step down into the open-air room holding the kitchen on one side, and the living room on the other.

"Like twenty-something, but I stopped participating in them after I won the one you just saw the portrait for. It started getting crazy, girls ripping or smearing lipstick on dresses that cost thousands of dollars, breaking high heels just enough that they wouldn't collapse until they made it up on stage...just cattiness I didn't want to be a part of. It wasn't fun anymore. So that's when I got into rock climbing my freshman year of high school. That was a lot more enjoyable than being around a bunch of snotty girls wearing six pounds of makeup."

I look out onto the screened-in back porch, and sure enough, there sit my mom and granny in the rocking chairs, sipping from mason jars of sweet iced tea. *So cliché, right?*

I open the left French door and step out onto the porch, looking back at Aiden when he follows me. The look of awe on his face is almost comical as he sees my backyard. After my dad retired from the Navy, he started his own landscaping business. The man doesn't just mow lawns and trim hedges. No, he designs beautiful gardens that can flat take your breath away, and he spared nothing when it came to our own property.

We live on several acres of land, with a small lake in our backyard we affectionately call 'the pond.' It was a spring-fed stream that my grandfather widened into a sizeable body of water, built the dam and several piers around the perimeter, and stocked it with fish. I grew up here, so it amuses me when new people get their first look of what I've seen since I was born. I guess I take it for granted, and catching the expression on their faces makes me remember for a little while how lucky I am to have grown up somewhere so beautiful.

"Well, there you are, KD girl," Granny says, still rocking gently in her chair, her silver hair shining in the sunlight making its way through the screens. She and Mom have always called me by my initials. Mom gave me Granny's name as my middle, Dorothy.

I force a smile to my lips as I introduce them. "Mom, Granny, this is the guy I was telling you about, Aiden. See? I told you he'd bring me back in one piece," I joke.

Aiden walks over to them and sticks out his hand for them to shake, and when Granny takes it in hers, she looks up at him and says, "He better be glad, or I would have found him and given him a ride on my foot." She cocks one grey eyebrow and glares her still-beautiful blue eyes up at him before letting go of his hand and taking a sip of her iced tea.

He laughs nervously and backs up to stand beside me, where I'm leaning against Granny's deep freezer she keeps all her freshly shelled butter beans and peas in.

"Did y'all have fun?" my mom asks, trying to soften the tension in the air.

"Yes, it was really pretty down there. Not too hot yet," I reply. I look over at Aiden and ask him, "You want to take a walk around?"

"Sure. We'll make it quick. You look like you could use

some rest," he says, and then follows me as I unlatch the lock on the screen door and make my way down the brick steps into my yard.

"We'll be back in a few," I tell Mom and Granny, and then we start the tour. I show him the gazebo in the center of one of the huge flowerbeds filled with azaleas, shaded by several large oak and pine trees. We take the stone path leading out of the garden that opens out into a giant grassy area, and walk down the slope of the hill to the part of the lake we call 'the beach.' Here, there is sand under the water, but if you go too far to either side of the area, or too deep, the floor of the pond is what we've always called 'greenies,' slimy underwater plant-life that's always given me the heebs when I'd accidently step into it.

We take off our sandals and step into the warm water, and I watch happily as Aiden sloshes over to where a swarm of minnows are swimming by the lily pads. He slowly lowers his hands into the water, trying to grab one, but they jet away from his closing trap. When he steps farther into the greenie-filled area, I smile genuinely when he picks a water lily, bringing it up to his face for a deep inhale of its sweet smell.

He splashes back over to me and hands me the white flower with a grin on his face. It's one of my favorite scents, and I thank him quietly as I keep it up to my nose so I can breathe it in for a while as we step out of the water and make our way over to the closest pier. Our paddleboat is tied to the front of it, but I don't really have it in me to go on a boat ride. Thankfully, it must've just rained, because the seats are full of water, and with no towels in sight, cleaning the seats off really isn't an option. If Aiden asked to go get one, I'd simply tell him we could go next time.

He doesn't though, obviously seeing how tired I look, and we climb back up the hill on the opposite side of the yard so he can see into our acres of woods next to our house. Hiking and four-wheeler trails are visible through the trees, and when he asks if we have an ATV, I tell him we don't but my cousins at the other end of the woods have a couple, and my uncle on the other side of the water has a golf cart. I explain the property is like a Brown family compound. Several of my mom's brothers—she has six—have their homes surrounding the lake.

When we get back up to the house, I walk past the screen door to the other side of the yard, so Aiden doesn't think we're going back onto the porch. I'm ready for him to leave so I can go up to my room and sleep after I call Anni and fill her in on what happened at the beach. He yells his goodbye to my mom and granny, and after showing him one of the gardens in the front yard, we make our way over to his car.

He pulls me to him for a hug, and I relax into him, knowing I'll soon be able to collapse on my bed upstairs. He tucks his hand under my chin and lifts my face to his for a quick kiss on my lips.

"I had a great weekend with you. I hope we get to do that again soon. I know you're exhausted, so I'll call you tomorrow. We can make plans to go dancing on Wednesday again or something," he says quietly.

I nod and squeeze my arms draped around his waist a

little tighter in response. When he loosens his grip on me, I let go of him and take a step back as he opens his car door and slips inside. "Bye, *girlfriend*," he tells me flirtatiously.

Obligingly, I reply, "Bye, boyfriend," attempting the same tone he used. He closes his door and starts his engine, and I give him a small wave as he pulls away, a sigh of relief leaving me as his car disappears down the road.

Chapter Seven

Kayla's Chick Rant & Book Blog

July 11th, 2005

I start my new job today. My friend Jenna has been working for GNC for over a year now and told me they were hiring for the store on base at the PX. She said I should make quite a bit of commission if I got the job, because all the soldiers shop there for their workout products. I went in for my interview last week, meeting Casey, my new boss, and instantly hit it off with her. She hired me on the spot and asked if I could start training the next Monday, today.

I'm pretty excited. It's a lot different than any other job I've ever had. I've never been in retail before, but I've always loved working customer service. I somehow have a way of making even the most disgruntled of people leave in a much better mood. I'm a good pacifier I guess.

A few weeks ago, I basically moved in with Aiden. Not officially, but if you go by the fact that most of my clothes are here now, and I've only been home a few times to visit my family, then I'd say I've sorta moved in with him. It started out the weekend after we got back from the beach. I went for the party that Friday night, stayed the whole weekend with him, and then left Monday to go back to my parents' house when he left for work.

The following weekend, I did the same thing, only Aiden asked if I'd mind picking up a few groceries for him before I went back home, since he hadn't had time that weekend. He gave me his key and debit card with his pin number, and didn't even flinch when I joked I was going to go on a shopping spree. He only grinned and shrugged, and then wrote me out a short list of the things he needed to make lunches and dinner for the rest of the week.

An urge to please him came over me at the grocery store, which surprised the hell out of me, having not had that feeling since leaving Texas, now months ago. I got everything on Aiden's list, plus some ingredients to surprise him with a home-cooked meal.

When he got home that evening, he was pleasantly stunned to see I had a dinner of chicken fettuccini alfredo and garlic bread set up on his small, round wooden dining table in his kitchen. When he leaned over the table and took a big whiff, he turned to me and swooped me up into his arms before setting me back on my feet and kissing me hard on the mouth. I smiled up at him as he told me he liked not only coming home to dinner already cooked, but also having his beautiful girlfriend waiting for him after a hard day of work.

The sentiment warmed me. I felt appreciated, and I was glad I had made the effort. I fought the dark thoughts trying to wiggle into my mind, making me wonder what it would have been like if Jason had asked me to stay in Texas, if this is what the end of the day would have looked like if we had moved in together like I had dreamed about.

I was determined not to let the thoughts bring me down, since I was feeling somewhat content with how my relationship was going with Aiden. Yes, we were moving very fast, but it felt like a natural progression, and everything was on him. He was the one who asked me to stay the night with him all the time. He was the one who told me I should just start keeping some clothes over at his house, so I wouldn't have to keep running home to change. It was him who took me to Wal-Mart and had an extra key to his house made, even stuck it on my key ring himself.

It was him who started taking care of my responsibilities, paying my car payment, my insurance, paid for all my food, and for everything whenever we'd go out. I tried to pay for things, insisting he at least take some money for my share of groceries, but I would find the cash I'd thrust into his hands back in my wallet the following day.

So I did what I could to make myself feel better about the situation, so I wouldn't feel like I was taking advantage of him, even though I knew I wasn't. I still felt guilty. I cleaned the house while he was at work, even though it hardly ever got dirty, since his roommate was deployed. I fixed him lavish dinners every night, and I made his lunches to take to work with him. I pleased him with my body every night. Anything I could do so I wouldn't feel like a kept woman.

But it got stale after a couple of weeks, just hanging out at his house all day while he was at work. Brittany went to school during the day, and Anni worked, so it wasn't like I could just hang out with them to pass the time. That's when I reconnected with my friend Jenna, and during one of our long phone conversations, she told me about GNC hiring.

A job. That's what I needed!

So after the long four-day weekend for Fourth of July with Aiden, watching the elaborate fireworks display on base, I called the store at the PX and set up an interview with Casey after Jenna had called her to give her recommendation.

I leave in about an hour, so I'll let y'all know tomorrow how my first day went! Wish me luck!

CHAPTER Eight

I'm gonna live like tomorrow doesn't exist

September 2, 2005

About two weeks ago, Aiden found out he was on the list for the next deployment. We knew it would eventually happen, seeing how he normally got deployed twice a year for four months at a time. I considered it fated I moved home and went to that party during a time he was actually home. I was definitely bummed he would be leaving, because each day I spent with him, it let a little bit of light back into the darkness I felt inside. But I'm not too worried about it. I love my job, and it keeps me pretty busy. When I told Casey my boyfriend is deploying soon, she asked if I'd like to work more shifts, and I gladly accepted. We closed at seven in the evenings, so Anni was excited I'd be able to spend more nights hanging out with her since I wouldn't have Aiden 'holding me hostage' as she put it.

It's true. We don't really go out as much as before, spending most nights at house parties near where we live so we wouldn't have to make a long trek home while intoxicated. Oh no, that hadn't changed. Getting drunk was a near nightly event, and I haven't even turned twenty-one yet. That's tomorrow.

When he found out he was deploying, he put in for a week of leave and invited me to drive up to Michigan with him to meet his family. The trip has pulled double-duty, because it's also my birthday tomorrow, and apparently in Canada, you don't have to be twenty-one to drink. Aiden is taking me to a casino across the Canadian border, that way he can take me out for my birthday and get to drink himself, since he doesn't turn legal until December.

We got here a couple of days ago. Having driven straight through, we ended up arriving around two in the morning. His dad met us at the door, and after a very brief but pleasant introduction, we went straight to bed. I adore Aiden's stepmom, Brandy, who has gone out of her way to make me feel welcome in their home, but I've actually spent most of my time playing with their two dogs: Rocky, a massive black lab who likes to play with his knotted rope, and Thor, the biggest damn Great Dane I've ever seen in my life, who also happens to think he's a little lap dog. He comes up to me and sits his butt in my lap, his giant paws still placed on the floor.

Their house is on Lake Huron, so right out the back door and down a small hill is the water. Last night, we made a fire and sat in camping chairs, talking well into the late evening hours. His dad isn't very interactive. He's spent the entire visit talking cars and football with Aiden, but I don't blame him, knowing his son is about to deploy. He did tell me it was really great seeing Aiden with a girl though, because he hadn't brought anyone around since his prom date years ago.

Today, we went horseback riding at one of Aiden's old friend Amy's ranch. I'm personally deathly afraid of horses, but I relaxed a little when Amy told me she was giving me her 'sweet old man' to ride. She said he's the one she always puts children on whenever they visit, because he is slow and friendly.

She didn't ride along with us, instead staying behind when the vet showed up to pull one of her other horse's teeth. So that left Aiden and me to ride around her huge ranch on our own. I have to admit it was pretty romantic. He moved his beautiful black horse close enough alongside mine that he could hold my hand, while I held onto the saddle with the other for dear life.

When we returned from our trip around the peaceful and lovely landscape, I hopped off the old animal and actually thanked him for being a good boy, giving him a tentative pat on his nose and then hurrying away before he decided to turn around and kick me.

Aiden took me to White Castle for dinner, because I told him I'd never had the mini cheeseburgers before. We just got back to his parents' house, and I am already ready for bed.

We snuggle up in his old bedroom and watch some TV, but when he tries to make a move on me, I turn him down flat, saying it would be too weird to do it not only in his parents' house, but especially with them home.

I find this quite funny, in a depressing kind of way. I never had any problem having crazy amounts of sex with Jason in his parents' house, even when they were home. Sure, they were always asleep, and most of the time didn't even know I was there because we'd arrive after a night out well past their bedtime, but they were still there. Maybe I just don't want to be intimate, and am using the setting as an excuse. Either way, we watch one last skit on Comedy Central before falling asleep, the image of Jason and me quietly sneaking through his house for a quick but passionate romp in his bedroom after a night of drinking and playing pool, mixing in my mind with visions of an idealistic horseback ride with Aiden.

After going through hell trying to get into Canada—they didn't like the fact we only had our driver's license and his military ID, instead of passports—we have finally made our way to the casino.

I've had a pretty fun birthday. We spent the day down by the lake, drinking wine and beer next to the water, and his stepmom brought us the best pizza I've ever had. She made me laugh, saying it was a pie, which was as close to a cake as I was going to get from their family, because she doesn't bake. That was fine with me, because it was absolutely delicious, and when I asked where she had gotten it, she told me it was from a family owned restaurant up the road that had <u>a fire oven</u>, which is what gave it such an amazing flavor.

We got ready for our night out, him dressing in a close-fitting grey polo shirt that hugged his biceps like a dream, with nice dark jeans, and I got dolled up in a short green dress and heels, earning a long whistle from Aiden when I walked out of the bathroom after straightening my hair.

As we walk into the casino, I look around in awe. The place is gigantic and loud, overwhelming every one of my senses. People are hustling around, buying drinks, turning in their chips for cash, or trying to find the slot machine that might spit them out thousands of dollars.

"What do you want to do first?" Aiden asks, looking around until I see him spot the poker tables.

"Well, it's my twenty-first birthday, so how about a drink?" I suggest.

"Let's do it, pretty lady." He takes my hand and guides me through the crowd toward the bar, and then orders me the drink I always get while we're out. Kyle introduced me to the snakebite while we were at Little Reno one night, where you could order the lemonade-tasting drink by the pitcher instead of just by the glass. It was yummy and went down entirely too easily, so of course it became my drink of choice.

Aiden hands me my glass of snakebite after telling the Canadian bartender the ingredients—who looked at us with a face that read 'weird-ass Americans'—pays for our drinks, and then swipes his bottle of Bud Light from the bar top. We make a lap around the perimeter of the casino, refill our drinks, and then settle at a set of Wheel of Fortune-themed slot machines.

"I traded some cash for this roll of Canadian quarters for you. This is what you'll have to use in the machines. Are you sure this is the one you want to play?" he asks, handing me the cardboard tube of silver coins.

"Yes, playing with real money at the poker table makes me queasy even just thinking about it. I'll stick with slots," I reply, expecting him to play the machine next to mine. But to my astonishment, he stands, leans down, quickly kisses me, and starts to walk away. "Aiden?"

"Yeah?" He turns back to me, but glances over his shoulder to where a game of Texas Hold 'em is going on.

"Um...where are you going?" I inquire.

"Well, while you're playing your slots, I'm going to play some poker," he says, obviously too distracted by the card game to realize the incredulous look on my face or the not too subtle amount of steam beginning to escape from my ears.

"By myself?" My eyes dart between the throngs of

people around us and Aiden, who still isn't catching on to my change in mood.

"Oh, you're fine, baby. I'll be right over there, see? You can see me from your seat," he says, pointing to the blue felt-covered table.

I sit there seething in my chair. It's true I'm not comfortable being left in a foreign place alone, but what's really pissing me off is it's my birthday! Why the hell would a man take his girlfriend out for her birthday, and then leave her to go off on his own? It's not like we came with friends, and he was going to play a game of poker while I hung out with my girls or something. No. I'll be sitting at a slot machine by myself like a damn gambling addict getting her fix. I imagine gambling like drinking—if you do it alone, you have a problem; it's meant to be done with company.

I don't even know how to communicate what I'm feeling without the possibility of causing a scene, so I just shake my head slowly while shooting daggers at him with my eyes, and growl, "Whatever," turning back to the Wheel of Fortune game I'm seated at. Having never had a girlfriend before, it's not surprising Aiden doesn't catch one of the words listed as 'danger words' that come out of a woman's mouth. He turns and hurriedly makes his way to the remaining open seat at the poker table.

I glare down at the roll of quarters in my hand, let out a long sigh, and begin unrolling one end of the coins. I've never seen Canadian money before, except for the occasional copper coin that's been mixed in with some similar looking pennies. On one side is the queen, and on the other is an animal…I can't tell if it's an elk or a moose. I know Aiden's game is going to take a while, so I only put in one quarter at a time to play.

I've replenished and lost my whole roll of coins twice since Aiden left me at the slot machine over an hour ago, and I've gone through a myriad of emotions ever since. I've fumed, admonished myself for being bitchy, justified my outrage, and have now slipped into a depressed state of defeat. By the time he finally comes back from his game, I'm ready to go to his parents' house, pack up my shit, and walk to the airport to catch a flight home.

"You done, baby?" he asks, excitement evident in his voice. It makes me want to punch him in his throat.

"I think so," I say in a tone that to any normal person would be evident I mean more than just the slot machine I've been hanging out with.

But of course, Aiden is totally ignorant. "Great, let's go turn in my chips for cash." He grabs my hand and pulls me to the cashier. As we stand in line, I look longingly over to the bar. My glass has been empty for an hour now. The waitresses hadn't come by the slots, but I had seen them refill the poker players' drinks several times over.

When it's our turn to trade in the colorful clay chips, I discover Aiden had won quite a bit of money, and would be bringing home a few thousand dollars more than what he came with. He puts the bills into his wallet, stuffs it into one of the back pockets of his dark blue jeans, and takes my hand once again, and we escape the loud and bright atmosphere inside the casino out into the quiet evening outside.

I get into the car, fully expecting to start making our way back across the bridge into the United States, but instead, he turns in the opposite direction. "Where are we going?" I ask with a sigh, weary over the thought of staying out late somewhere I don't know, being left alone once again. This trip has taken a wrong turn. My birthday had started out so good, and I wish we would have just stayed at the lake instead of coming out.

"It's a surprise," he tells me, giving me a conspiratorial grin. I let out a huff of air and turn toward my window, watching the darkening scenery pass by.

A few years ago, I went to visit my boyfriend at the time, where he lived in Anchorage, Alaska. He was based at Ft. Richardson in the Army. I spent my Spring Break there, and the place was absolutely majestic. I always thought Canada would be the same, for some reason, and maybe it is in other parts, but here, just on the other side of the border, it looks no different than the northern states. I don't know why, but my brain just envisioned that as soon as you crossed into Canada, it would be some beautiful winter wonderland. Must be the time of year, or something.

We pass plain looking buildings and several restaurants, go down some sketchy looking streets that have my heart fluttering, and finally pull onto a main road that leads us to a bar. Aiden parks the car and hops out, then I see him turn to look at me through the windshield when he realizes I'm not following him like a happy little puppy. He comes over to my side and opens my door, but I don't immediately get out.

"You coming, birthday girl?" he asks with a smile.

"This is my surprise?" I ask with a cocked eyebrow.

"Well, not the bar itself, but what's inside," he explains.

With a dramatic sigh, I unbuckle my seatbelt and take his hand, and after he slams my door shut, he pulls me inside the building.

The bar is nondescript, nothing special, just a hole in the wall bar like any other. He tells me to pick a booth for us while he goes to get us some drinks, and I pick one toward the back, where I see a sign leading to the 'Smoker's Deck.' Something tells me I'll need it to be close by.

The hostility that had waned into a silent broil is now back, and I really just want to go home. And then to add to my queue of emotions, sadness decides to join the party, because the thought, *Jason would have never left me alone on my birthday*, pops into my head, followed by, *Yeah, he'd just leave you...period.*

Period...

Hmm, I wonder if that's my problem. Am I PMSing right now? Is that why I feel like I could totally snap and become one of those people on some TV show about a woman freaking out and chopping everyone up into little pieces? No clue. And I don't really give a fuck right now.

Aiden returns with our drinks and starts chattering away.

Oblivious. I have never met a person so absolutely unobservant in my life. Either he's completely clueless to the female way of passive-aggressively saying 'you're a fucking douchenugget' because of his lack of past relationships, or he purposely just chooses to ignore it.

As I sit here visibly fuming in my chair, my arms crossed over my chest, my right leg crossed over my left, with its foot wiggling at the speed of light in my fury, he continues his one-sided conversation as if I'm happily chatting along with him, when all I'm really doing is giving him a death glare. Oblivious.

I'm not even really listening to what Aiden is saying until I hear the words "about to deploy," and it snaps me out of my anger just long enough to start paying attention to what he's talking about.

"...and I was wondering what you thought about maybe doing what Brittany and Chris are going to do before his next deployment," I hear the end of his sentence.

"What?"

"Brittany hasn't told you?" When I shake my head, he explains, "Before Chris deploys on the next trip, he and Brittany are going to get married." At my startled look, Aiden pushes forward, "Well, it's obvious that's what their relationship is leading to, so why wait? Before he leaves, he'll be able to make sure she's got everything she needs, everything from the extra money it puts in his paycheck to insurance, and then she'll also have access to everything on base without the hassle of getting searched every time. All the gyms, the commissary and PX, the family center, which will definitely be helpful when dealing with a deployment. They have support groups and shit. It gives a guy peace of mind while he's in the desert, not having to worry if his girl back home is okay."

He looks from my face to where he pulls one of my hands out from where it was smashed between my arm and my side.

"So what are you saying?" I ask meekly, a mix of emotions roiling through me. Fearing he means what I think he means, panic at what my reaction will be when he clarifies, and maybe even a little bit of...excitement?

"I'm saying...or rather I'm asking...do you..." He licks his lips and shifts in his seat as he squeezes my hand. "Do you want to get married?"

My jaw drops and all I can do is stare into his beautiful eyes. He looks so hopeful, so nervous. I don't know what to say. Only thirty seconds ago, I was so pissed off at him for ditching me at the casino I could have dumped him right there, but now he's asking me to marry him?!

He starts rambling, "I'm sorry I ran off at the casino to play. I couldn't tell you what I was doing then, but I was making a wager with myself. I told myself if I won enough money in two hours to buy you a ring, then I would ask you to marry me. If not, and I lost, then I would take it as a sign I was insane and forget about it. But, I won! I won enough to buy you pretty much any ring you could want...well, from like, Zales or something. Not like Tiffany's or wherever the hell it is with the rings as expensive as a fucking house."

I can't help but giggle at his outpouring of word vomit. And after hearing his explanation of why he'd even consider it okay to leave me alone on my birthday, I can't help feeling like a total bitch for getting so pissed at him for it.

"I..." I begin, but nothing comes out. I need to think. Marry Aiden? I mean, everything he just said about the benefits is absolutely true. It would make life a lot easier. But...do I want to marry someone because it would be convenient?

"I need a cigarette," I state, standing abruptly. He sits back in his chair and lets go of my hand, looking disappointed. "I just need a minute to think, Aiden. This is coming out of nowhere. Give me ten minutes by myself without you looking at me with those puppy dog eyes. This is a big decision you're springing on me."

"I can give you that," he concedes, and I feel his eyes burning into my back as I make my way out onto the patio outside.

It's a little chilly out in the dress I decided to wear tonight, but luckily, there are tall, silver heaters scattered around the deck. I take a seat next to one, pull out my menthol cigarette and pink lighter, and take a much needed inhale of the nerve-calming smoke.

Marry Aiden? I repeat inside my head.

For some ungodly reason, a scene from one of my favorite movies, *The Sweetest Thing*, pops into my head, when Christina Applegate's character tells Cameron Diaz's, "And if it doesn't work out, you could always get divorced."

I snort a laugh to myself. I haven't even decided if I'll marry him yet, and I'm already planning an escape route? Good sign, good sign.

I shake off the aggravating thought and try to make a mental checklist of the pros and cons of saying yes.

Pro: Everything he said about Brittany and Chris—the extra money, the insurance, access to all the facilities and support on base.

Con: Knowing in my heart I'd be marrying a dude for convenience, even though that's technically how he just tried to sell himself.

Pro: A guy actually wants to marry me. And not just a guy, a really good one, who treats me well and does everything I always wanted Jason to do.

Con: Knowing I'll be marrying someone who is just a replacement for the one I really want. He may be scarily similar to the love of my life, but he's not *him*.

Pro: I can actually see myself marrying Aiden. I can see myself being content as his wife.

Con: We've only known each other a few months. Is that really enough time to know someone enough to marry them?

I weigh both sides of my list, and after taking a giant swallow of my drink and the last drag of my cigarette, I sit up straight, square my shoulders, and then stand.

When I slide myself back into the booth, Aiden looks like he's about to come unglued he's so nervous. I decide just to put him out of his misery, telling him with one nod, "Yes."

"Yes?" His voice goes up an octave higher than I've ever heard it before, and it makes me smile.

"Yes, I'll marry you, Aiden," I spell it out for him.

"Holy...holy *shit!*" he shouts, and I see the few patrons of the bar and the bartender turn to look at us. "She said *yes!* I asked her to marry me on her birthday, and she said yes!"

Everyone in the bar claps, and I feel my face heat up. I know I should be feeling a lot happier about everything—this is not how the heroines in my books feel when they get their happily ever after and their heroes ask them to marry them—but this is reality. I've come to realize my books are fiction. Book boyfriends aren't real. They're written for fantasy, to escape reality and dream of things that don't really happen.

And with that depressing thought in mind, Aiden comes around to my side of the booth, pulls me out of my seat, and dips me in a long, passionate kiss that would've had any other woman's toes curling in her shoes.

Me? I'm just grateful when it ends and the bartender hands me a congratulatory drink on the house.

Two days later, when we drive back home, we stopped by Kyle's house and brought home an eight-week-old kitten. She was all black with green eyes. When Brittany had told us her and Kyle's cat, Jager, pronounced like the liquor, who now lived with Kyle since they broke up, had kittens, I'd wanted one so badly, but Aiden told me no; he wasn't a cat person.

I knew it was bribery to cheer me up, or maybe his form of an olive branch or apology for leaving me alone in the casino. In the end, I forgave him, because now I had my Jade, someone to pour my love into while my soon-to-be husband is deployed. Maybe she'll be enough to distract me, to keep that evil voice from coming back in my head.

CHAPTER Nine

Phone's blowin' up, they're ringing my doorbell

September 7, 2005

    I hear the phone ring from where it sits on Anni's bed. I'm in one of her metal dining chairs in her kitchen, where she is currently highlighting my hair. She's closing up one of the foils after lathering the strands inside it with bleach, since I've been talked into lightening my hair because Anni told me a change might do me good. And as she pinches it shut, I hop up from my seat and bolt into her room, trying to catch the call before it stops ringing.

    I don't even take the time to look at the screen to see who it is before flipping it open and asking a breathless, "Hello?" pushing back a couple of foils that have flopped onto my forehead and over my eyes. The voice that comes over the line makes my heart immediately jump into my throat, and I close my eyes.

"Kayla?"

God, that voice. That deep, soothing, Texan accent pours over me like warm cream. The months I've gone without hearing it had not faded the memory of it, and I still heard it in my dreams nearly every night, except for on the nights I was either too exhausted or had passed out too drunk to dream.

Tears well behind my closed lids, and I can't make myself respond, so it isn't surprising when he asks, "Are you there? Kayla? Is this still your number?"

"Jason?" I breathe. That's all that can come out. The name I haven't spoken aloud in weeks, not even to Anni, escapes from my lips, sounding like someone long dead had just called me from the other side.

"Hey, babe. What's up?" he asks, like a day hasn't passed since the last time I saw him, like he hadn't gutted me and left me for the vultures.

I stumble back into the kitchen and my legs give out underneath me just as I reach the chair I'd been sitting in only moments before. I look up at Anni through my water-rimmed eyes and see her mouth, 'You okay?' before Jason starts talking again.

"What you been up to? How was the move?" And that's when I hear it, the light slur to his words as he asks the questions. Jason drunk-dialed me.

I glance at the time on the microwave sitting on the

kitchen counter and see it is four in the afternoon my time, which means it is only three in Texas. Why is he drunk in the middle of the day on a Tuesday?

"Hey, Jason," I say quietly and move my eyes back to Anni when I hear her sharp intake of air. When she starts storming toward me with her arm reaching out to take my phone from my ear, I hop up from my chair and get behind it, putting it between us as I hold my hand up to stop her. "The move was fine. Everything is...fine. How have you been?"

"Oh...I've been all right, I guess. I miss you a lot," he tells me, and the first of many tears finally escapes my eye.

"I miss you a lot too." I pause. "How are your parents? They doing good?" My heart is pounding so hard I can feel it moving the fabric of the frumpy T-shirt Anni had me put on before she started dyeing my hair. I can hear my pulse in my ears as I listen intently for the sound of the voice I've missed more than anything.

"They're good, they're good. Well, I'm drunk as fuck and just wanted to tell you I love you. I'm a fucking idiot, and I love you. There's a dumbass out in the world that loves you, just so you know. That's all I wanted to tell you, so...yeah."

Sucker-punched. Right in my solar plexus. I can't breathe. I can't move. I can't think of anything but the words 'I love you' in Jason's voice repeating itself over and over as it twirls and dances inside my head. How long had I ached to hear those words from him? Dear God, I think I'm going to pass out.

"Kayla? You there?" I hear from a distance. It sounds hollow, and I realize I'm no longer holding the phone up to my ear.

"Why? Why are you saying these things now? Why are you doing this to me?" I wail into the receiver.

"Babe, what's wrong? I'm not doing anything to you. I just wanted to tell you I love and miss you. That's all." He sounds confused, like he really can't understand why calling a girl whose heart he shattered to tell her he loves and misses her would not be a very kind thing to do just out of the blue.

It infuriates me, and the anger at him I had pushed aside resurfaces. Wanting to hurt him as much as he hurt me, back in Texas, and now, confessing these feelings, with as much venom in my voice as I can muster, I spit at him, "Well, you should have thought about that before you just threw me away, Jason. I miss you, and God knows I love you, too, but you can't fucking do this. I'm getting married."

Silence. And then I hear the flick of a lighter and a deep inhale as he pulls smoke into his lungs, letting it out slowly through those perfect lips I can still visualize as clearly as if I could see them right in front of me now.

"Married? To who?" he finally asks.

"His...his name is Aiden, and he's good to me," I reply, not knowing what to say.

"We only broke up like four months ago," he says, the hurt I was trying to inflict evident in his voice.

"Broke up? Jason. We were never officially together. You never asked me to be your girlfriend. You never called me yours. You used me and then just tossed me away when you were done with me." I begin to cry, and this time I let Anni take the phone as I crumple to the floor in a heap, sobbing so violently I don't even hear what she says.

Kayla's Chick Rant & Book Blog
September 19, 2005

Today was my wedding day. We woke up early and got to the Lillington Courthouse right when they opened, Brittany and Chris tagging along as our witnesses.

We told my family what we were planning about a week ago, letting them know we were just going to do a quickie ceremony at the courthouse, but then we want to do a 'real' wedding when he gets back from deployment. My mom said in that case, she'd just wait for the real one. She thought it was too soon to be getting married, but having been around Aiden a lot more in the past couple of months, she had really grown fond of him. She also liked the fact I'd be moving back in with her while he's deployed.

There's no sense in me staying by myself, us paying rent while he's gone, when I could just move in with my parents and save up all the money. Then, when he gets home, we can go apartment hunting. This weekend, we'll be moving all his things—which isn't very much besides his clothes, a dining table and chairs, and some kitchen stuff—into our little shed next to our house, and then a few days later, he'll deploy for the next four months.

I found the ring I wanted yesterday. I was at the mall with Anni and walked into Reed's, and when I spotted it, I knew it was the one. I always knew I wanted a pear-shaped diamond, and this one was so pretty, with a pear in the center circled with tiny diamonds, and then a few down the sides of the band. The wedding band matched, but was way different than anything I'd ever seen before. It was two white gold bands that were attached to each other, and the engagement ring slid in between them, making it look like one whole piece.

I called Aiden at work and told him what I'd found, and he told me to go ahead and get it, and to find him whatever wedding ring I wanted him to have. He couldn't have anything too fancy because of work, and he'd more than likely be wearing it on a necklace anyways, since it probably wouldn't be too safe wearing rings while working on airplane engines. So, I chose a white gold band with a small bevel detail down the center, simple, but not boring.

The ceremony wasn't anything special. I dressed in a pretty coral, floral-patterned dress, and he wore a shirt of the same color. We first went into the clerk's office and filled out the marriage license, immediately followed by the magistrate's office, where we said our vows. After a brief, awkward kiss in front of the stranger, Brittany and Chris signed the marriage license, and then we left to go get some lunch. Aiden went to work a few hours later.

Now, I know what you're really wanting to know. What happened after my last post, when I told y'all about Jason calling me—thank you for the comments of complete outrage by the way, and to whoever asked the ever-important question if my highlights turned out okay, yes, they look awesome!

I couldn't exactly go home to Aiden looking like run-over dog shit after crying over another man for two hours, when Anni was finally able to stop all my blubbering. God love that woman. Even in my hysterics, she managed to get my foils out, wash, and even tone my highlights, finishing off with a deep conditioner. All the while I was a limp ragdoll bawling my eyes out.

Jason had ripped open all the wounds that had just begun to scab over. And that's when Anni brought out the big guns, also known as a giant bottle of wine. I guzzled that shit like it was water...well, like water for normal people. I can't stand water. Squirrel!

So as I focused on keeping myself upright on the stool in her bathroom as she blow-dried my hair, she talked me down in her mystical Anni way, and when she drove me home, I only looked semi-crappy, with fabulous hair. Aiden asked me what was wrong, and Anni made up an excuse on the spot, saying she had made me watch a Nicholas Sparks movie. She's my hero.

CHAPTER Ten

It's my fault to think you'll be true. I'm just a fool.

Aiden's been deployed for exactly one month today. I've kept myself pretty busy with work and hanging out with Anni and Brittany so far, so it hasn't been too bad. The day of his deployment was a pretty emotional one.

We got up early and loaded all his rucksacks into the car, then went to the airplane hangar on base that his plane would be leaving from. The place was huge; I had never been in a hangar before, and the wide-open space was hollow and depressing in itself. There were rows and rows of bench seating, where families were gathered, waiting for the time to say goodbye to their loved ones for the next four months.

Aiden and I sat on one of the benches near Brit and Chris, where we held hands and I rested my head on his shoulder, breathing in his clean scent through the odor of engine oil and jet fuel. Despite not being madly in love with him, he is still a comfort to me. I do love him; it's hard not to in some way, shape, or form. He's just a really good guy, funny, and can be so charming at times. I'm content with him, which is more than I could've thought possible after my experience with Jason.

So when it was time for Aiden to get into formation with his fellow airmen, it was with genuine, heartfelt sadness I gave him one last long kiss goodbye, hanging onto his hand for as long as I could before he let it go when he walked to the other side of the hangar. I watched with tears in my eyes as they played the national anthem, listening as their commanding officer gave a speech and led a prayer that they'd all come back safely.

I've missed him while he's been gone. I even made a countdown on my blog for when he comes back, picking a roundabout date, since they can't tell us for sure when they'll be home. We email each other every day, and I talk to him on the phone about once every three or four days.

The three of us girls go out dancing at least once a week, and I take pictures of myself to send Aiden in my emails. At first, he loved the pictures, telling me how beautiful I look, but lately, he's been...off, and the phone conversation I'm having with him right now just proves my uneasy feeling.

"We went to South Beach tonight," I answer after he asks me what I'd been up to today.

"Again? Y'all go like every week," he remarks, an annoyed tone to his voice. I'm not going to apologize for or stop hanging out with my friends. We all love dancing, and South Beach is the only place in town that plays decent music, so that's where we regularly go.

"Yeah, that's our place. We never get messed with while we're there, and the bouncers know us now and always keep an eye out for us. You have nothing to worry about," I reassure him, thinking his concern is for our safety.

"I got the email a couple hours ago, from when you were getting ready with Anni to go out. Is it really necessary for you to dress like that?" he asks testily.

I look down at my hiphugger jeans and my white crop top I'm still wearing, since he called right when I walked in my door after coming home from the club at one a.m. I'm dressed like every other girl who goes out dancing. Actually, I'm far more covered up than most of them. Some girls show up in low-cut dresses that barely cover their butt while they're standing, so you can bet your sweet ass when they dance and bend over, they are showing all their goodies.

"I'm wearing jeans and a shirt, Aiden. I'm not out there flashing everyone my pussy in a miniskirt. And you've been out with us before. You know I spend most of the time sitting at a table drinking, and only get up to dance when my favorite songs come on. Shit, we don't even get there 'til nearly eleven, so we're only there for a couple hours as it is," I huff.

"Why do you have to wear makeup? Who are you trying to look good for?" he inquires, and that is the absolute last straw.

"Are you fucking kidding me? When have you ever

seen me *without* makeup? I'm a girl! I'm twenty-one, and I care about the way I look. I'm not going to go out into public looking like shit. I dress up and put on makeup for myself, not for anyone else, because I like to feel good about myself. Where is all this shit coming from, Aiden? You're pissing me the hell off with this insecurity bullshit. I have never done anything to deserve all this interrogation," I practically yell, trying not to wake up my parents down the hall.

After a pause, he finally speaks up. "I'm sorry, baby. One of our guys just found out his wife cheated on him the week after we deployed. A fucking week. He was only gone seven days when she went out and found someone else to fuck. It's just messing with my head."

I know deployments can be hard for both the guy and his significant other back home. There are bad days, and there are good days, and I feel bad his friend got cheated on and put that little nugget in Aiden's head, but that's no excuse to freakin' talk to me like that.

"I'm sorry for your friend, but you have nothing to worry about. If you think that's something I'd do to you, then that's really fucked up. I thought you knew me better than that. Why would you ask me to marry you if you thought I'd cheat on you the moment you left the country?" I snap.

"I know you wouldn't. It's just…I miss you, and being over here gets lonely, when all I want to do is be home with you, curled up and watching a movie or something. It's only been a month, and I'm already going crazy without you. I've been on a ton of deployments, and I've never had anyone waiting on me back home before. It's much…different. Way harder than I thought it was going to be," he confesses.

Maybe it's the drinking I did at the club, but his words don't affect me the way he probably thought they would, and I reply, "Well snap the hell out of it. Think of how cool it's going to be when you get back, when we get to go pick out an apartment that's all our own. Just stay busy; that's what I'm doing. I miss you too, but I'm trying to keep my mind off it."

We talk for a little while longer, until he's back to his normal upbeat self, and when we hang up, I barely have the energy to change into pajamas before I pass right out. It's my normal nightly routine, the only way I've found not to lie awake thinking about dark brown eyes and perfect lips that never failed to make my heart race, something it hasn't done in a really long time.

Kayla's Chick Rant & Book Blog
December 12, 2005

What is it they say about boredom? An idle mind is the devil's playground? Well, ain't that the damn truth. And MySpace is the fucking merry-go-round. Why? Why did I get on the damn search feature? Why did I type in *his* name? I was just asking for trouble. What the hell is wrong with me?

I wasn't expecting Jason's name to come up. He doesn't seem like the social media type. Of course, he did have the Plenty of Fish account, so maybe I shouldn't have been surprised. I'm sure lots of people use MySpace as a dating site; I mean, that's how I found Carson before I met Aiden. I just use it to find old friends from high school nowadays.

He's got a plain black background, but all his lettering is neon green, and he has "Aerials" by System of a Down as the song playing on his page. The profile picture he has chosen is of him sitting at his parents' dining room table with some friends I don't recognize, playing cards, with Ramen Noodles hanging out from between his lips. Even as stupidly silly as it is, I couldn't help the tears that sprung to my eyes at seeing his face for the first time in seven months.

I clicked on the picture, bringing up his different albums. There were several of him with a white hardhat on his head, and there was heavy machinery in the background. There was one of him on the floor with a black cat, and he was smiling up at the camera. The smile made my heart hurt, and I forced myself to click out of the pictures before I came across something that might've killed me.

I went back to his main page and looked through his About Me.
Name: Jason Robichaux
Location: Houston, Texas

Star Sign: Aquarius
Birthday: January 25
Marital Status: Single

I stopped right there, though. That's all I really wanted to know, if he had found someone else yet. Not even thinking about it, I clicked on the button to follow him.

I haven't gotten a notification saying he added me yet, and I'm sitting here freaking the fuck out, thinking about what I've done.

That was such a dumb idea.

The next day, after obsessively checking my MySpace, and totally stalking Jason's profile, I finally get the notification I've been waiting for. Jason added me to his friend list. And not too long after, I receive a private message from him.

From: Jason Robichaux
Wow, long time, no speak, stranger. How have you

been? How is the married life? I see your husband...weird... is in the Chair Force and is deployed right now. You getting along okay? I've got a really good job for a company putting together windmills. They send me all over the place. It's pretty cool, and I'm in charge of projects that cost millions of dollars. Can you believe someone put me in charge of that much money? Yeah, me neither.

Anyway, sorry about that phone call a few months ago. The next day, when I woke up with a hangover from hell and remembered what I'd done, I felt like a complete asshole. I haven't called back, because your friend Anni is scary as fuck. That girl can make a man's ballsac shrivel in fear.

Anyway, I hope to hear from you. I do miss you like crazy.

Jason

My heart pounds as I read and reread his words over and over. It's like no time has passed. Unlike his last phone call, I'm not filled with anger or devastation. But it does bring back every feeling that's lain dormant for the past few months. Him talking about my husband makes me cringe, making me feel...embarrassed almost. I sit back in my computer chair, wondering how to respond, and after a few minutes of mulling it over, I decide just to wing it.

From: Kayla Lanmon
Hey there!
Building windmills? How did you even come across a

job doing something like that? And no, I can't believe they let you play with millions of dollars. They better audit you to see how much of that goes toward Shiner and cigarettes. I bet that takes up quite a chunk.

The deployment is going good. I'm staying busy. I work at GNC, the nutrition place, and I'm living with my parents until he gets back. I hang out with Anni all the time, and I have lots of reading time, so it's actually passed pretty quickly. Hard to believe he already gets back next month.

I miss you, too.

Kayla

I proofread my message to him before I send it, fixing a couple of typos I made in my haste to talk to Jason, and press the send button.

I feel a little guilty talking to him when I'm married to someone else, but when I think about it, I know lots of people who are friends with their exes. Maybe that's what we could be. Yes, I would give anything to be with him, but I know he doesn't want that, so I'll be happy with him in my life in any way. He was my best friend in Texas before we started sleeping together. There's no reason we can't go back to the way things were. Or at least, that's what I tell myself.

CHAPTER Eleven

Sometimes I wish she was you. I guess we never really moved on.

Over the next two months, Jason and I message each other back and forth like a ritual. It feels like we're the old Jason and Kayla, before the confession he made about liking me since the day he met me, when he told me he didn't really like large women. I update him daily on what I'm up to, almost like he's a diary who actually responds. He confides in me just the same. I haven't told anyone about our correspondence. I can't help feeling it's a dirty little secret, but I always justify it to myself by saying in my head we're just friends. It doesn't matter the love I had for him has grown exponentially over our emails. It's not like I've flown to Texas to fuck his brains out...even though I've fantasized about it nightly.

The usual face-splitting grin returns every time I see I have a message from him waiting in my inbox.

From: Jason Robichaux
December 28, 2005
I am so sick of the beer in Iowa. Wish you'd fly out here with a pack of Dos Equis to split with me. But don't forget the lime and salt. You don't like it plain.

Get this: I wanted to go out to a nice restaurant one night to break up the monotony of fast food and mom-and-pops places here in the boonies, and when I asked where I should go, the dude told me, "Oh! We have a really nice restaurant up the way there. But you gotta put on your Sunday best. You can't miss it. It's called Applebee's."

I don't know what I laughed at more, his accent, or the fact he thought I needed to put on my Sunday best for a fucking Applebee's.

Save me.

As the weeks pass on, writing each other every day, we get comfortable again, talking about anything and everything, even asking each other advice, me about Aiden, and him about random girls he decides to go out on dates with. It makes me vomity thinking about him with other girls, but I have no right to be jealous, when I'm in NC fucking married to another man.

From: Kayla Lanmon

January 16, 2006

Aiden comes home tomorrow. I'm excited to go apartment hunting! I've always wanted a place I could make my own, decorate it however I like. I've been collecting all sorts of stuff since he left, to have to put up on the walls and make our place pretty.

I wonder if it's going to be awkward between us, after having not seen each other in four months. He's still being weird. He's been questioning every single thing on our bank account, from how much I spent at the club on drinks, to every single item I've bought at Wal-Mart or at the mall.

At first, I would go along with it, using it as conversation during our phone calls, telling him about the new outfit I found or the cute throw pillows I picked out for the new apartment. Conversations with someone in the desert get really boring after a while. I mean, they can't really talk about what they are doing over there, and you're just going on with your usual mundane daily life, so the call usually goes like this:

Him: Hey, what did you do today?

Me: The usual. What about you?

Him: Same ole, same ole. I miss you.

Me: Miss you too. Only *insert number of days* left until you get home.

Him: Yep, I'm excited.

Me: Me too.

cricket chirp, cricket chirp

But then it started getting really annoying when he'd want to know exactly what I bought at the grocery store, like he's waiting for me to confess I bought extra-large condoms and an economy sized bottle of lube so I can go out a-cheatin'.

I thought I'd be smart and just cash my paychecks and use the money to go about my business, but he noticed I hadn't deposited it right away. I told him I just hadn't made it to the bank yet.

I don't know. After the whole blow up over me wearing makeup, and now all this craziness over what I'm spending money on, I'm feeling like the walls are closing in on me. I don't like being controlled...unless I'm naked. *snort*

Yeah, okay. Maybe I shouldn't be talking to Jason—or any friend in general—over marital things like bank accounts, but I couldn't keep it to myself any longer. I need some advice, and not the kind given by counselors on base, who would no doubt take the side of the person deployed. They'd give me psycho-babble about what they're going through over there, when really, there's no excuse for Aiden's controlling behavior.

What had happened to the sweet man I married, who months before we got hitched had given me his debit card and told me to buy whatever? It's not like I was out spending money irresponsibly. I'm a very frugal person. I always shop sales and use coupons, and I don't buy extravagant things. And I'm buying things for us, for *our* apartment, to make it a home. The one thing I buy myself that I don't feel is a necessity are my books, and those are actually pretty vital to my sanity. But even those I buy at Edward McKay's, the used bookstore my mom and I have been going to since I was a little girl.

From: Jason Robichaux
February 6, 2006
Have you gotten all moved in yet? How's all your frou-frou girl shit look? I know you were excited about decorating. Hope he's chilled out now that he's been home a couple weeks. Makes me a little crazy thinking you're over there miserable. All I want is for you to be happy.

My friend Alissa and I are getting an apartment together. That'll be weird. Not because she's a girl or anything, because she's like a sister, but because I'll have my own place. I won't be there very often. Maybe for about a week at a time once every couple months, since I work out of town all the time. It's mostly because she needed a place to stay but couldn't afford rent by herself, so I figured why not.

Can't wait to see some pics of your new digs. I'll send you some of mine when I get moved in. I'm sure it won't look as good as yours though.

I can't help the bit of jealousy that fills me thinking about Jason living with another girl. He's told me about Alissa, and I totally believe there is nothing between them, but still. I remember how hopeful I'd been that last time I saw him, driving down to Friendswood, believing he was going to ask me to stay in Houston past my semester of school. My mind had run rampant, imagining Jason and me moving in together.

After I get my kitchen and dining room all decorated, I snap a few pictures and send them to him. I've covered the walls in everything I could find that was Irish-themed, from four-leaf clover dangling lights that circle the small dining area off the kitchen, a metal wall sign that says Irish Pub, and I even found some neon beer signs. It may not be Irish, but I couldn't help buying the glowing green Dos Equis sign I hung in one of the corners.

All of my kitchenware is green. It might be cheesy, nowhere near classy-looking, but we're young and it's fun. I have plenty of years ahead of me to turn into a Stepford wife with floral patterns and lace.

After seeing everything put together, Aiden loved all the stuff I'd bought. He apologized for being crazy while he was away, and chalked it up to missing me so much and wanting to be home. I told him I forgave him. But in my mind, I knew I'd never forget.

From: Kayla Lanmon
February 20, 2006
You're going to think I'm such a nerd...or maybe you won't. I remember you and Gavin talking about Day of Defeat *all the time. I'm totally into a video game! Aiden got a PlayStation while he was in the desert. I think he said his dad sent it to him for his birthday in December in a care package. Anyway, I was getting really annoyed when all he'd want to do is come home from work and play it all night, so he went out and got this game we could both play. It's called* Champions of Norrath.

You just go around these worlds and kill shit, leveling up and buying more powerful weapons and armor, but what's cool is you play as a team, not against each other. It's much better than just sitting around watching him play crap I have no interest in.

How did the date with that chick go? Was she as cool as she seemed on MySpace?

Apparently, she is. Jason and I still write back and forth to each other, but not as often. Between him working and dating this new girl, I get a message from him maybe twice a week at most, when I had been used to talking to him about twice a day. We hadn't actually spoken to each other on the phone since that day in Anni's kitchen, but the messages had been like a lifeline. I could reread them while I waited for his next response.

Without his letters to look forward to every day, I slip back into old habits, drinking every night with Aiden and his friends, when before, I'd just go to bed early while he stayed up and hung out with them. Our apartment was hardly ever empty. I guess making my dining room look like a pub wasn't the brightest idea I ever had, accidentally creating a party place for everyone to come hang out when they didn't want to go to a bar or club.

Aiden and my relationship is...weird. It's like we're roommates with benefits or something. Not what I imagined married life would be like. Every day is always the same. We wake up around eleven, he goes to work from noon to eight, and I go to work from two to seven. Getting off an hour ahead of him, I get home and make us dinner, and we eat it on the couch while we either watch a movie or play our video game. If one of his friends doesn't come over, we usually stay up pretty late just the two of us, or I'll go to bed while he stays up to play by himself.

On the weekends, it's just the same as it was before he deployed. Party, party, party. Either at a friend's place, or out at the bar. I'm actually grateful for it now, with the thought of Jason seeing another girl, being so into her he doesn't hardly writes me anymore. When he does though, I cherish every word. And I value every word of advice he gives me when I write him with a problem.

From: Kayla Lanmon
May 13, 2006
I am so fucking pissed off right now!!! How many times have I read one of my steamy books and pranced around naked in front of that asshole, trying to pull his attention away from that goddamn PlayStation, only for him to ignore me, not even LOOK at me. And do you know what I just found? Aiden. In the bathroom. Sitting on the fucking toilet. Looking at porn on his phone and jacking off.

Seriously? We were in the middle of watching a movie we rented, at two in the afternoon on a Saturday, and he said he'd be right back. He was gone a while, so I went back to check on him, make sure he was okay, and I opened the door and he was fucking cranking one out! I grabbed his phone out of his hand and looked, and he has pictures on his phone of blonde-haired, big-breasted skanks from porn sites.

I don't know what pisses me off the most. The fact he was doing it in the middle of the day, when we were in the middle of watching a movie together, what the girls look like who he fantasizes about—which is the complete opposite of flat-chested, brunette me—or the fact I make it obvious I'm here whenever he wants me, but he chooses to jack off.

He fed me some bullshit about being too tired to have sex, but still wanted to get off really quick. Oh, yeah, because it takes so much energy for you just to lie there while I do all the fucking work as usual. He had no excuse for the porn. He just stuttered and babbled incoherently.

Oh, my God, I don't even know what to do with myself right now.

I ended up pressing send and then crying myself to sleep in bed.

CHAPTER Twelve

For comfort, for solace, for the end of my broken heart

The next morning, when I wake up, Aiden is already up and ready for the day. He tells me to get dressed, that he is taking me somewhere. He won't tell me where. I'm not really in the mood for his bullshit, but I'll take any opportunity to get out of the apartment.

I'm surprised when he pulls into Anni's apartment complex, and when we pull up out front of her unit, I see her trot down the stairs, her big red purse slung over her shoulder. She opens the back driver's side door and hops in, and after closing it behind her she looks at me with a grin and says excitedly, "Let's go pick out your puppy!"

"What?" I look between her and Aiden, and then back

again, completely confused.

"Yeah, dipshit here called me last night asking what he could do to make up for some *indiscretion* he wouldn't give me details about—*you can tell me later*," she stage whispers. "I told him while he was deployed you couldn't wait to find an apartment when he got back, and the main prerequisite of said apartment was that it had to allow pets, because you wanted to get a dog. On your apartment's website, it just says the dog must be under twenty-five pounds, so we're going to the haven in Raeford to see if there's a furbaby you want to bring home," Anni explains.

"We're going to get a dog?" I ask, trying to process everything she just said.

"Yes! The only stipulation is you have to forgive the douchecanoe for whatever stunt he pulled yesterday," she tells me.

Oh, if I'm getting a dog, I can pretend to forgive him for being such a sleaze yesterday. I'll win the Academy Award for my acting skills if it means we'll go right now and pick out a furbaby. I love Jade, don't get me wrong, but she's a cat. You only get to love on her when she allows it. I want a dog so badly, whether it's a puppy or an adult. It doesn't matter to me, as long as it's mine and will snuggle with me.

I lunge across the center console and kiss Aiden's cheek, squeaking, "Forgiven!" before bouncing in my chair. "Let's go, let's go!"

He grins and puts the car in reverse, and then we start our trek to Raeford. It takes about forty-five minutes to get to the animal haven, and when we arrive they are just opening.

We park and get out of the car, and as we make our way through the gate, a woman walking a big mixed-breed dog greets us. "Hey there, folks. What can I do for ya?"

"We're here to find my new baby!" I practically shout. Thankfully, she finds my enthusiasm a good thing, and she asks what exactly we're looking for. "Well, we live in an apartment, and the only rule is it has to be under twenty-five pounds. I'm not one of those people who has to adopt a *puppy,* but I also don't want a senior."

"So what we call a teenager would be fine with you. Full-grown, but not about to keel over," she jokes.

"Exactly. I'm not picky on breeds. It can be a mutt for all I care, but I want it to be super affectionate. I want a lapdog for sure," I explain.

"Ooooh, I think I have the perfect pup for you. You just wait here and I'll go and get the little fellow," she tells me with an excited gleam in her eye.

I stop her before she goes. "What kind of dog is it? I'm just curious."

"He's a sweet little Chihuahua. You're just going to love him!" she says, and then hurries off with the large dog in tow.

I turn to Anni with a sneer on my face. "A Chihuahua? Ugh, I don't want a little rat. I want a dog."

"Well, you told her you didn't care about breed," she reminds me.

"Yeah, I guess. I just meant I didn't care if it was an AKC freakin' purebred show dog. Oh, well. Let her bring him out. It's not like we have to go with the first dog she shows us." I shrug.

As we stand around waiting for her to bring the Chihuahua out, I take in the haven around us. There is a giant barn directly in the center of the property, and we can hear dozens and dozens of dogs barking inside it. To the left is a smaller building, and if I'm not mistaken, that's where the sound of cats meowing is coming from. There is a big fenced in area, where I see a couple of horses milling around. As I glance in the direction the woman had gone, I see there are large wire pens that hold small groups of dogs. I can't tell how they are organized, because there is a mix of all sorts of breeds and sizes in each kennel.

A few minutes later, the woman returns carrying a tiny white dog, who is curled against her chest, shivering like it's below freezing outside and not the ninety degrees it is right now. When she approaches me, she turns him to face me, and I swear on my books, he has tears in his eyes. My face and heart melt instantly at the sight of him, and I reach out to take him from her. When I pull him against my chest, he wiggles up until he can bury his miniature face into my neck, and I'm done for.

"Oh, my God. This is my baby," I whimper, rocking the dog back and forth, stroking his back as I feel him sniffling against my throat.

"I had a feeling," she tells me with a nod.

"What's his story? Why would anyone get rid of such a sweet little guy?" I inquire.

"Someone found him wandering the woods in Ft. Bragg. Poor thing was about starved to death. It's a wonder some type of bird of prey didn't swoop him up. We don't really know where he came from, but the usual story is a soldier will either get deployed or stationed somewhere else, and instead of taking the time to find the animal a new family, someone to keep it for them while they're gone, or to bring them to the haven or the pound, they just let them go. I guess hoping someone will take them in," she explains.

"Well, that's just sad," I say quietly, still stroking the little furball. "Anything else you can tell me about him? Health and all that stuff?"

"Judging by his teeth and a couple other factors, we think he's around two or three. He's already neutered, and when you adopt from the haven, you get a package with Banfield Animal Hospital to get all his shots, since there's no way to tell if he's had them or not. He's not microchipped, but he seems to be in really good health, now that we've gotten him to a much better weight than when he was brought in. He's a little anxious. We put him in a kennel with much larger dogs, because for some reason the smaller ones scared him more than the big ones." She reaches out and scratches him behind his ear, and he wiggles closer to me.

"So where do I sign?" I laugh. I know this tiny creature is meant to be mine, and I'm ready to take him home.

"Wait, maybe we should see some other dogs before just choosing the first one with a sob story," Aiden interjects.

I turn toward him with a death glare. "We came here for *me* to pick out a dog," I remind him.

"Yeah, I know that, baby, but he's the very first one you've seen. We haven't even made it inside yet." He gestures toward the giant barn where the barking is coming from. "What if there's one in there you'd like even more than this... Chihuahua," he says with an unattractive look on his face.

"Look, when she said Chihuahua, my immediate response was negative. But look at him." I turn him to face Aiden. The little guy struggles to get back in the nook he's found against my body and I giggle. "He already loves me." I kiss the soft fur of his neck right below his ear. For some reason, the doggy smell there is comforting, and I hold him a little tighter. He doesn't seem to mind.

"Okay, hang on to him, but still, let's at least look at the others. Would that be all right?" he asks the employee.

"Sure! Who knows? Maybe you'll end up adopting more than one," she says teasingly, obviously recognizing from our conversation we're only here because my husband is in the doghouse. I snort at my own thoughts.

We spend the next twenty minutes walking through the aisles of kennels inside the barn, and sure, a few dogs make my heart melt, but none of them make me feel the way the tiny guy in my arms does. He's let me carry him like a baby the entire time, sometimes making adorable little sighs and doggy-moans of delight as I rub his belly or scratch his neck.

I've basically tuned everything else out, except watching Anni melt over dog after dog is quite entertaining. Unlike me, who's landed on my little dog soulmate, she can't decide between any of them. She wants them all. She eventually says if she could have any dog there, it'd be the gargantuan Saint Bernard who gave her a full body tackle-hug when the woman opened up his kennel for her, but she knows she can't have a dog that big at her apartment complex.

In the end, Aiden gives in. Not that he has a choice. The Chihuahua is mine. The haven only accepts cash or checks, so the woman tells us she'll go run the paperwork for us, while Aiden runs up the road to the gas station to use their ATM. I happily sit next to Anni on a swing to wait for him to get back, still snuggling the little white animal in my arms.

I try to get him excited, making my voice high-pitched and energetic, attempting to get him to play and be rambunctious, but he won't have any of it. He ignores me and buries himself under my shirt. Soon, his breathing evens out and he gets really warm, like a miniature personal radiator, and when I pull the neck of my shirt out and look down at him, he is sound asleep. I let him stay there with a goofy grin on my face, even as I feel sweat bead between my boobs and start to trickle down my stomach.

Aiden returns with the cash and we get all the papers signed. She gives us a packet of all sorts of coupons and goodies for dog stuff, and then wishes us a happy life with our new furbaby.

Heading back to Fayetteville, we all decide to stop for some lunch, and land at my favorite restaurant, Smithfield's Barbeque. We go through the drive-thru and park in a space to eat in the car, not wanting to leave the Chihuahua in the heat.

"So what shall we name you, little guy?" I pick him up out of my lap and hold him in front of my face. I could seriously hold him in one hand he's so tiny.

"Snowball?" Anni suggests.

"Nah, I don't want him to have one of those cutesy pet names. Let me think." I hum as I consider the animal in my hands. "Okay, he's a Chihuahua, so he's Mexican. But y'all know my obsession with Irish stuff. What's a good, strong Irishman's name?"

"Angus," Aiden calls out with his mouth full of French fries.

"Ugh, no. He's not a cow," I shoot down.

"Conan," Anni says.

"Hmmm...that's a good one. What else?" I tilt my head, looking at the dog.

"McNeil...McDougal...O'Connor...O'—"

"Riley!" I shout, interrupting Aiden's list of suggestions. "Riley. My little Irish Chihuahua. Oh! And I'll name you after Zorro, the coolest Mexican ever. I dub thee Riley Alejandro." I laugh and pull him to me, rubbing my face against his soft fur.

"Perfect," Anni confirms, and after tucking Riley back against the side of my leg in my seat, I grab my bag of food and devour my barbeque sandwich and fries, washing it down with the best sweet tea in the world.

God, I'd missed Smithfield's while I was in Texas. I can remember playfully bantering with Jason over who has the best barbeque, Texas or North Carolina. Here, barbeque means pulled pork in a vinegar sauce, and it's served on a hamburger bun and topped with coleslaw. In Texas, barbeque is beef brisket with red sauce. I could eat Smithfield's every day for the rest of my life. Nothing can top it in my book.

When we finish our food, I ask Aiden to take us to Petsmart. I'm excited to get all the new dog stuff we'll need for Riley. I sift through all the coupons the woman at the haven gave us, and see there's one for just about everything we'll need, from food to a doggy bed, and everything in between. When I'm done with this shopping trip, Aiden will think twice before sneaking away to jack off to porn when his willing wife is sitting right next to him.

Kayla's Chick Rant & Book Blog
July 3, 2006

I haven't heard from Jason in almost two months. I can see on his MySpace that he's dating a different girl than before, and it makes me wonder what happened. What happened to the previous chick he was dating? How did he meet this new one? Why did he never write me back if he wasn't too busy in between girlfriends?

These are the things I have time to stress and obsess over, because I literally have too much time on my hands. All

I do is go to work, come home, and go to bed. Aiden spends every minute he's not at work either playing his PlayStation, or online, his new obsession: online poker tournaments. And yet, he freaks out if I want to go hang out with my girlfriends. It's gotten to the point where I just said fuck it; I'd rather just read in bed than have another screaming match over me going out without him, since he doesn't want to come with me.

At least my blog is doing fantastic! Have y'all been able to keep up with all my reviews? I know I've been posting a shitload of them, so I hope you've found a few books that interest you. God knows I can barely keep my stash stocked I go through them so fast. Aiden tried, futilely, to tell me I needed to cut back on how many books I buy. He shut up that line of ranting when I picked up his fancy wireless PlayStation remote and threatened to throw it over our apartment's balcony, because if he spent money on frivolous shit like a controller for the ultimate purpose of being able to play his stupid-ass game, even when he had to go to the bathroom, then I would buy as many fucking books as I damn well pleased.

Without the letters from Jason, or the time spent with my best friend—who had tried several times to kidnap me, a couple of times succeeding, but the fighting the next day with Aiden wasn't even worth the effort—I became severely lonely, depressed, almost desperate.

If I was going to waste away inside my apartment, only allowed to spend time with my jerk of a husband, then dammit, I was going to be the best little housewife there ever was. Our apartment is always immaculate, our dinners are always delicious and pretty, and there is not a single thing Aiden can complain about, from his perfectly-pressed work uniform, to his homemade lunches, to his ever-present stock of snack foods he likes to munch on while playing his games.

It's gotten to the point now though that I feel like I'm one of those stage-five clingers. And so when I presented him with something I want, with the exceptional reason I gave, he jumped at the idea, ready to squeegee my ass off him so he could get back to his video games in peace.

I want a baby.

GASP! I know. I already had to hear an earful from my loudmouth bestie. It's not the greatest decision to have a baby because I'm lonely. But y'all know me. My little body is too small to contain all the love I have inside me. I want someone I can pour my overflow into. That baby will be the most loved, spoiled rotten little thing that will ever be brought into the world. All the attention I have to give someone that Aiden doesn't appreciate or even want, I will put into my son or daughter. And in return, I'll have someone who truly loves me, unconditionally.

I'm aware he or she will be mine, all mine, because I don't expect Aiden to change his ways, and in a way, if I do get pregnant, I wouldn't want him to. I'll have something that's all mine that he won't be able to keep me away from.

So, today, on my weekly run to Edward McKay's, Riley, my ever-present companion in his doggy-purse as usual, I didn't just scour the romance section. I bought every book on pregnancy they had.

Only bad part about trying to make a baby? Now I'll have to have sex with Aiden. *grumpy face*

Consolation: I'll just fantasize about my heated nights with Jason to get the juices flowing. Even though I'm hurt over Jason's disappearance, not a single bit of my feelings for him have waned.

If he were to message or call me right this moment, or any moment in the future, I'm sure we would pick up right where we left off, like no time had passed at all.

CHAPTER Thirteen

This distance, this dissolution. I cling to memories, while falling.

September 2, 2006

    I wake up with the all but forgotten feeling of being ran over by a Mack truck. Only I didn't drink last night. Believe me, I tried. We went to the pool hall for my birthday celebration, meeting up with a bunch of our old friends for a night out, away from the apartment—that's all I wanted.

    But, the moment I walked into the smoky bar, I had to rush back outside to puke my brains out. Was it the dinner I ate? I didn't know. But after I got it all out of me, I felt better, and we went back inside. Nothing alcoholic sounded good, so I just got a Sprite to sip on until my stomach settled, but it never did. Aiden didn't want to leave, all wrapped up in a game of pool with a few of his coworkers, so Anni ended up bringing me back home. Déjà vu, right? Another birthday I was left alone by the man—cough, *boy*—in my life. Is it normal for a husband to let his sick wife go home without him? It seems like that would be something one just wouldn't do.

I shrug it off. Whatever. I've given up caring what he does. Instead of dwelling, I roll myself out of bed and make my way to the bathroom. When I sit on the toilet and see the roll of paper is empty, I open the cabinet under the sink and reach in for a new one, and that's when I see the stack of pregnancy tests I bought at the Dollar Tree next to my box of tampons. I bought them when Aiden and I first started trying to get pregnant.

Doing a little math in my head, I realize I'm over a week late for my period. I immediately flex my muscles and cut off the stream as I snatch one of the tests from the cabinet, hurriedly rip it open, and read through the instructions.

After following all the steps, I prepare to wait the three minutes it says it'll take for the results to appear, but it takes less than ten seconds for the second little pink line to show up.

I take a deep breath.

I'm pregnant!

Elation fills me. I can barely contain my excitement. I jump up from the toilet, wiggle until I pull my pants all the way up, and then take a second to live in the moment. I stare at the test, tears filling my eyes as I grin stupidly at the lines like they're going to respond to my joy.

But all of a sudden, all that elation, excitement, and joy turns abruptly into nausea, and I throw myself back at the toilet, emptying out the little bit of Sprite I drank when I got home last night. When the shivering subsides and I feel like I can stand, I get up and walk out into the living room, seeing Aiden is passed out on the couch, the start screen of his video game repeating its opening theme over and over.

I walk over and turn off the TV, and the quiet wakes him up. He jackknifes off of the couch and then looks at me, and his red-rimmed eyes tell me he's probably still drunk from last night. I'm so glad he had such a good time without me at my birthday get-together.

But I don't let my irritation with him bring me down. I punch my arm out in front of me with the test facing him in my hand and announce, "I'm pregnant!"
He stumbles over to me and takes the white plastic into his hands and then looks from it to me. He smiles crookedly and then surprises me by wrapping me in a big hug.

When he pulls away, he says, "Some birthday present, huh?"

I grin and look down at the pregnancy test in his hands. "Yep, I got exactly what I wanted." I glance at the time on the cable box above the TV and see it's way later than I thought it was. It's close to noon, and thankfully I have the weekend off for my birthday.

We're meeting my parents at Peaden's Seafood Restaurant in a few hours for an early dinner. We've been going there since I can remember for special occasions. It's a pretty far drive from my parents' house, on the other end of Fayetteville, but our apartment is only about fifteen minutes away from it. So that gives me plenty of time before we need to start getting ready to go.

While Aiden goes to take a shower, I do a little research in my pregnancy books and on the Internet on the nausea I'm having. I make mental notes of all the tips they give on how to ward off some of the morning sickness, which I learn quickly is a liar of a name. I have all-damn-day-and-night sickness. I need to get some Saltine crackers and some ginger ale, and I discover there are hard sour candies with ginger in them that seem to work for a lot of women. I'll make sure to swing by Motherhood Maternity next time I'm at the mall to grab a container of them, since it looks like that's the only place you can find them.

After a little more research, I see a lot of people recommend Sea-Bands, which were first created for sea-sickness, but seem to work just as well for morning sickness. I'm not really sure how they work, a lot of talk about acupressure, but I'm willing to give anything a try.

I close up the laptop and bookmark the pages in my books, and then go into the bathroom to get ready to take a shower. Maybe that'll make me feel better until I can stop at a store on the way to dinner for some ginger ale. Aiden is drying off with one of our big, fluffy black towels, and I strip out of my pajamas quickly, ready to get under the hot spray. He catches me around the waist as I go to move past him to step into the tub, and I don't know if it's the motion of him swinging me into him, or the pressure of his arm against my stomach, but it sparks another wave of nausea, and I bend double over the toilet.

At first, he jumps back, surprised by my sudden sickness, when he was trying to be affectionate for once, but then he pulls my hair away from my face, holding it at the back of my head as he rubs my back. There's nothing left in my stomach, so all that comes up is burning foamy acid, the taste and smell snowballing the shittiness I feel. When my heaving finally ends, he helps stand me up, and I move toward the shower.

"You going to be okay to stand up in there by yourself? Maybe you should take a bath instead," Aiden suggests, sounding genuinely worried.

"I'll be fine. Just keep the bathroom door open or something. I'll call out for you if I need you." I don't know how I feel about his sudden concern. Ever since he got back from deployment, I would swear he doesn't give two shits about me. This new side of him makes me uncomfortable. I think I'd rather just take care of myself, without his help.

But instead of leaving and keeping the door open like I asked, to my horror, he lowers the lid of the toilet and takes a seat. "What are you doing?" I ask, irritated.

"You look like you could faint at any second. You're all shaky and pale. I'm not going to leave you by yourself and let you, like, pass out in the tub and crack your skull open," he says sternly.

"Wow, way to make a girl feel pretty." I roll my eyes and close the clear shower curtain, and as I wait for the water temperature to feel just right, which doesn't take long since Aiden just got out a few minutes earlier, and I turn on the showerhead, I see him grab the nail clippers out of the basket on the counter and start cutting his nails.

The situation feels so...domestic. A concerned husband sitting close by clipping his nails, while his pregnant wife showers. If my feelings for him were stronger, this would be a moment I'd treasure. This would be a moment I'd look back on and tell my son or daughter, "Your daddy was so sweet. He didn't want to leave my side for fear I'd get hurt while I was pregnant with you. Such a protective husband."

But instead, I'm annoyed. Where was this Aiden for the past year we've been married? All I've known for the last year, through his deployment and since he got back, has been some selfish, domineering, controlling asshat. I've gotten used to that person, and it weirds me out he can all of a sudden just up and change his whole personality.

Or maybe I'm just being a bitch. Didn't I just read in the pregnancy books that the hormones running through my body could give me crazy mood swings? Should I be more appreciative of his behavior?

I don't know. And at this moment, I don't really care. All I know is the shower is making me feel much better, and I can't wait to get to the restaurant to tell my parents they'll be grandparents for the seventh time over.

In sorrow, I speak your name, and my voice mirrors my torment

"It's going to be a girl," my mom states matter-of-factly, making me laugh.

As we waited for our food to arrive, sitting in our wooden booth at Peaden's, my dad and me devouring the delicious hushpuppies—the cornbread feeling fantastic on my empty stomach—dipping them in ketchup like we've always done, I announced that I was pregnant. Seeing my excitement in the way I told them, they knew to be happy for me. Mom knew I was trying, so she wasn't surprised by the news.

Daddy reached his hand across the table and shook Aiden's hand, who just shrugged. *Yeah, that's right. Just shrug like it's no big deal, because it's not one for you. You just got your rocks off*, I think hatefully.

Mom made her proclamation of the baby being a girl, snapping my attention back to her, and I laugh. "Oh yeah? How do you know?" I ask.

"Well, just think about it. Your brothers, from oldest to youngest, had a pattern. Mark had two boys. Tony had a boy then a girl. Jay had a girl then a boy. So, boy-boy, boy-girl,

girl-boy...the only pattern left is girl-girl. I bet you a million dollars you'll end up having two little princesses for me to spoil rotten," she tells me with a nod and an adorable giddy glint in her bright blue eyes.

"A million dollars, huh?" I tease.

"Yep. Your momma knows these things." She smiles, and my excitement grows at the elation in her eyes. My mom and I have always been super close. I've always heard the term 'daddy's girl,' but I am definitely a momma's girl. She and my granny are my favorite people in the entire world.

It's just been us three gals against all the boys. Besides my dad and my three older brothers, I also had six uncles around all the time, four who lived right around our lake, one down the road, and one who visited from Minnesota every chance he got. I don't know if that's why my granny, mom, and I have always been so close, me being the only little girl, but I wouldn't have it any other way.

"Well, in that case, Jocelyn it is," I inform the table.

"What?" Aiden prompts.

"Ever since I was fifteen, I always said if I have a girl, her name would be Jocelyn. It's the name of the princess in *A Knight's Tale*. I heard the name and just knew that'd be my daughter's name," I explain. "And there's no point in even trying to argue with me. Her name will be Jocelyn, whether you like it or not."

Aiden glances at me with a surprised look on his face, and I feel heat slide up the back of my neck, not embarrassment, but a want for him to even try to voice a negative opinion about the name I've loved for the past seven years. *Bring it.*

"You know what? I kind of like it. It's different, and that movie is badass. Jocelyn it is," he wisely agrees. "On the off chance your mom is wrong, do you have a boy name picked out?"

"I was toying with names, combining a couple, playing with the spelling, and I got the best idea when you mentioned maybe naming him Aiden Jr., when we first started trying a couple months ago. But I wouldn't want to deal with the confusion of having two Aidens, so I came up with Avan. I combined Aiden with Ava, my mom's name, and got Avan." I look at my dad across the table as he dips another hushpuppy into the ketchup. "He'd be Avan Michael."

My dad looks up at me and grins. "That's an awesome sentiment, baby girl. But you know your mother is never wrong. Jocelyn is a beautiful name."

"Then it'll be Jocelyn Ava," I confirm, and when I see tears fill my mom's eyes and watch as she grabs her napkin to dab at her lashes, I lose it. My mommy never cries, and from the beaming smile on her face, I know they are happy tears. Aiden wraps his arm around my shoulders as I half-sob, half-laugh along with my mom.

When our food arrives, the waitress doesn't know what to think. She places the plates in front of each of us and then hurries away after asking if we need anything else. Mom and I compose ourselves, and when I look down at my plate, my stomach growls angrily. I'm starving, but the thought of putting even one of the fried popcorn shrimp into my mouth makes the nausea return full force.

Mom must see my discomfort, because she quickly grabs the tinfoil wrapped baked potato off my plate, cuts it open, adds a little butter and some salt, and then mushes it all up inside its skin. She pulls the plate out from in front of me, removing the overwhelming fishy smell from directly under my nostrils, and replaces it with the fixed potato. She hands me a fork and then scoots my Sprite closer to me.

"Small bites, KD. Take a small bite of the potato, and then a sip of Sprite, back and forth," she instructs, and I cautiously do what she said.

Shockingly, I make it through my potato, and then finish off the leftover half of Aiden's and the hushpuppies, the heavy carbs and the tingling carbonated beverage making my stomach feel comfortably full for the first time in two days. I should've known my mom would have the solution. After all, she had four of us.

When Aiden and I get home, he goes straight to the couch and turns on his laptop for a round of Texas Hold 'em on his online gambling site. I shake my head in exasperation, but also smirk with relief. I should have known his concern and affectionate behavior wouldn't last long.

I go change into some pajamas and slide beneath my down comforter, feeling full and tired, like I could sleep for a week. I pull my laptop over my legs from my nightstand and open up the document I was using to toy with baby names and their spelling. Yes, I'm one of those people who want to spell their kid's name all weird. Sure, they won't be able to buy personalized stuff off the shelf, but more and more places are popping up where you can get things customized, from decorative license plates to embroidered towels, so I'm not concerned.

I type out my girl's name.

J-O-C-E-L-Y-N.

And I don't know if it's because it's in all caps or what, because I'd never noticed before this moment, but an idea dawns on me, and I feel a surge of adrenaline when I type out the name for the first time.

J-O-S-A-L-Y-N.

Besides the L-Y, if you rearrange the letters, it spells Jason. I'd give just about anything to wake up and this all be a dream, waking to realize that I'm happily married to my soul mate, and the doctors were all wrong and we were able to make a beautiful baby. But I know this is my reality, and for once, knowing I'll have my baby to love, I feel a sense of completion when I type out the rest of her name, and end up falling asleep with a secret smile on my face.

My daughter's name will be Josalyn Ava.

Kayla's Chick Rant & Book Blog
November 8, 2006

    I broke our TV remote throwing it at Aiden's head yesterday when it missed and shattered against the wall beside him. It was worth missing my target just to see the look on his face when I actually did what I threatened to do. Motherfucker.

    We found out a couple of weeks ago he was deploying again. Trust me, this was fine by me. The inconsiderate prick needed to go away. For me, the day I found out I was pregnant, it was an easy thing to immediately stop smoking. I haven't picked up a cigarette since. Especially with all the morning sickness I've had, the smell of cigarettes was an instant trigger for my nausea. One would think that if a man knew the smell would make his wife, the woman carrying his unborn child, miserable and barf her brains out, he would stop that shit. Oh no, not Aiden. His response? "You're the one who's pregnant, not me. Why should I have to quit?"

    Cue the giant silver cable box remote zooming through the air and missing my mark by mere inches, plastic, rubber buttons, and batteries flying in all directions.

    After that, he finished packing up all his stuff in his rucksacks and started loading up all the boxes I've been packing into the moving van. I'm going to stay with my parents again while he's gone. I've absolutely had it with him. As far as I'm concerned, he's just my sperm donor and roommate.

Something else one would think? When the plan is for your pregnant wife to go live with her parents when you deploy in a few weeks, you don't make her—who has dwindled down to a mere 93 lbs., because all she can keep down are baked potatoes and Preggy Pops—pack up the entire apartment, while you sit on your ass and play video games. The thirty or so boxes that fill our living and dining rooms have all been packed by yours truly. Not a single one was filled by the jackass I have the pleasure of calling my husband.

Dear God, only three more days and I'll be rid of him. I won't even have to spend Thanksgiving, Christmas, or, most importantly, New Years with him. Thank goodness, I'll get to spend my favorite holiday in peace.

CHAPTER Fourteen

And, yes, I've dreamt of you too.

November 20, 2006

    I sit in the waiting room of the OB/GYN office in Womack Army Medical Center, my leg bouncing up and down excitedly as I wait for the nurse to call me back. I'm exactly sixteen weeks along.

    My mom and Anni are with me for this special day. We're here to officially find out the sex of the baby, even though we all already know it's a girl. We just know. Finally, my name is called, and the three of us follow the young nurse back into one of the exam rooms. The nurse takes all my vitals, and after looking at my record, she breathes a sigh of relief when she sees I'm starting to gain weight.

    It was seriously mind-blowing. The exact day I moved

into my second trimester, the morning sickness abruptly stopped, replaced with an overwhelming hunger I had never felt before in my life, along with a craving that wouldn't stop. McDonald's McRibs. And just my luck, the damn things weren't available yet.

McRibs are only available for a limited time every year. But the demanding little thing growing inside me would hear none of it. My only choice? I actually called McDonald's. Yep, I called them and pestered them until they finally gave in and told me when the secret release day of the McRib would come this time. And thank you, baby Jesus, it was only in a week. I could hold the little mongrel off until then, distracting her with chicken nuggets dipped in BBQ sauce.

The second the clock struck 10:30am on the day the McRib was released for the season, my happy ass was in line at McDonald's with what I'm sure was a scary, ravenous look in my eyes as I stepped up to the register and ordered one.

My mom and I sat down at a table, and as she ate hers at a normal pace, I devoured mine in three bites. I hopped up from the table, BBQ sauce still covering me from one cheek to the other, and ordered two more. Those were gone in minutes. Mom watched me with wide eyes, and I could tell she was trying to hold in laughter as she handed me a napkin. I wiped my mouth, let out a relieved groan, spun my butt sideways in the booth, and lay down on the bench seat. It was the best day I'd had in a long time.

The nurse tells me it'll only be a few more minutes until one of the ultrasound rooms would open up, and we could just wait here until then. True to her word, only a little while later, she comes and gets us, leading us to a curtained off area of a dark room. She pulls over another chair to sit beside the one next to the padded table I'm about to lie on, and Anni and Mom take their seats, the excitement evident on both of their faces.

"Okay, Miss Kayla, just hop up there and roll your pants down as low as you are comfortable with, and pull up your shirt to just under your breasts. Your technician will be right with you," the nurse tells me, and then leaves, pulling the curtain closed behind her.

I do as she told me to, exposing my little bump, and I rub it in wide circles. "All right, baby. It's show time. No hiding the goodies, okay? Make Mommy proud." I'd read in one of my parenting magazines that sometimes the baby could be in a position where you couldn't see their private area. I'm so excited, and have been counting down the days until this appointment. It would be devastating not to get a glance, confirming I'll soon have a little princess. I've been holding off buying anything for the baby until I know for a fact she's a girl.

The technician calls out, "Knock, knock," and I let out an anxious laugh, telling her to come on in. She takes a seat on the high, rolling stool next to the sonogram machine on the other side of me, and gives me a big grin. "Are you excited? I'm excited. This is my favorite appointment during a patient's pregnancy," she says happily.

I like her already. Nothing is more frustrating than being super excited about something and the people around you being party poopers. "I'm dying. Let's do this!" I plead.

"Eep! Okay. I'm just going to squirt this on your belly, but we've got these new fancy warmers now, so it's nice and heated, not painfully cold like it used to be," she explains, shaking a white bottle above my belly before squeezing a large amount onto my lower stomach. She sits it to the side and grabs the wand, sticking it into the glob of clear goop.

Soon, the loud, fast sound of my baby's beating heart fills the room, and just like the first time I heard it, and at the following couple of appointments I've had since I found out I was pregnant, tears fill my eyes. I look over at my mom and see her wide smile.

"Alrighty, let's give this little one a photo shoot," the technician says, more to herself than to me, as she sits closer to the screen and pushes buttons on the keyboard. The image switches to a much closer angle, and she turns down the volume of the heartbeat.

I watch fascinated as the baby comes into view. You can see her little hands are up next to her face, and we can even see it when she opens her mouth wide, like she just yawned.

She moves the wand to the left side of my belly, wiggles it a few times to get the baby to move a little, and that's when we see it. Drawing an arrow on the screen, the technician types out G-I-R-L. As plain as if my daughter is lying right here in front of me, we see her little hoo-ha. My mom was right. Josalyn Ava it is.

The technician says she's going to take a few more pictures to have on record for measurements, to keep track of her growth, and all I can do is nod. I'm overwhelmed with the knowledge I will be the mother of a beautiful little girl. I knew she'd be a girl. It was just a feeling, even if my mom hadn't said anything and put it in my head. But actually seeing it, observing that she's clearly got female parts, it fills me with the most wonderful emotions I've ever felt. For the first time in my life, I feel complete. As long as I have her, I won't need anything else in the world. Anything else good that comes along will just be icing on the cake.

Chapter Fifteen

You know me all too well. My only desire, to bridge our division

Thanksgiving, 2006

I've been thinking a lot about Jason lately. It's weird. I mean, he's always in the back of my mind. Every day, something reminds me of him, whether it's a song on the radio or a memory that just happens to pop into my head. So it's extra creepy when after spending all day helping my mom and granny cook Thanksgiving dinner, and then enjoying it with practically my whole family, I get a call on my cell phone. The caller ID tells me it's *him*.

My heart jumps into my throat, and my hand shakes as I press the send button and lift the phone to my ear. When I go to say, "Hello," my voice catches, so I clear my throat and try again, this time succeeding.

"Hey there, beautiful." Oh, dear God. That voice. That perfect, deep, rich, Texas-accented voice. My knees buckle beneath me, and I plop down on the side of my bed.

"Hey, Jason," I breathe. "Happy Thanksgiving." I'm so proud of myself for getting the words out.

"Happy Thanksgiving to you, too. How are you feeling?" he asks.

His question confuses me. I haven't heard from him in six months. Although we've remained friends on MySpace, he's never commented on one of my pictures or anything. Has he been keeping up with my profile? Does he already know I'm pregnant? He answers my questions without me having to voice them, as always, knowing exactly what I'm thinking.

"I've looked at every picture, read every comment and note...I know you're having a little girl. I've wanted to message you for so long, but with you being pregnant, I thought you were finally happy with Aiden, and I didn't want to mess anything up," he confesses.

"Then why are you calling me now?" I question quietly.

"I just...had a feeling. I felt like I *needed* to call you. I know it sounds weird, but something just told me I should call and check on you. Are you okay? Everything going all right?" he asks, and I can hear the genuine concern in his voice.

"Yeah, I'm fine. Aiden is deployed again, so I'm actually better than before," I tell him.

"Wait, what?" he asks, confused.

"Aiden and I are anything but happy together, Jason.

Yeah, I'm having a baby girl. I'm so," I let out a heavy sigh, "so very happy to be having a baby. But the circumstances aren't what you think."

"Tell me about it, babe. God, I've missed talking to you. Just unload. Tell me everything," he prompts.

And I do. I tell him absolutely every detail of what's been going on since his MySpace messages stopped coming. I even send him the links to my blog posts so he can read anything I might've forgotten in my outpouring of the last six months.

And just like that, I have my best friend back, and exactly like I thought, it's like no time has passed at all.

From: Jason Robichaux
December 8, 2006

I remember kind of blowing you off when you asked me a long time ago about me wanting kids. You said you saw on my old Plenty of Fish account that I wanted them someday, but then I told you I couldn't have any. I don't think I ever got around to telling you why I can't.

I was like eleven or twelve when it happened. I was at the park—you know the one off FM2351 before you get to my neighborhood? I was there with a group, Boy Scouts or a church thing, I don't fucking remember. What I do remember is riding my bike, and then all of a sudden the most excruciating pain I've ever felt hit me right in the nuts. Like, forget what it feels like to get kicked in the balls...not that you know what it feels like...but multiply what you think that feels like by about a million.

I was on the ground holding my junk and crying, and my buddy ran over to me to see what was wrong. All I could do was tell him to call my dad. At the time, there were no cell phones or anything, and he was a friend I played with regularly, so he thankfully had my number memorized. He got on his bike and hauled ass down the road to the gas station and called my parents.

When my dad got there only a few minutes later, he picked me up and put me in the truck. I thought I had just wracked myself with my bike or something, and that the pain would just go away, so he took me home. But before we got there, the truck heater caught on fire, filling the whole cab with smoke. By the time we got home, the pain had doubled instead of lessened.

My mom kept asking me what was wrong. I was in so much overwhelming pain that I cussed her out. I used every profanity I'd learned up to that point, but through the cursing, she was able to make out that something was really wrong with my balls.

This is the part that pissed me off. There are so many fucking hospitals and urgent care clinics within just a couple miles of where we live. And yet, my mother made Dad drive all the way downtown to Texas Children's. At the time, I thought she didn't care I was in so much pain. Couldn't she hear me screaming at the top of my lungs in the back seat? In the end though, I'm sure it was for the best, since I had to have surgery.

When they finally got me to the hospital, my dad picked me up again and ran into Emergency. All my parents could tell them was I was having severe pain in my testicles.

They got me back in a room, and when they pulled off my jeans and underwear, I watched as my dad seriously got ghostly pale. I don't know why I remember that, and how he couldn't be in the room after he saw my balls were literally blue. Not the metaphorical kind.

Anyways, they immediately gave me morphine for the pain. I remember I kept seeing a bunny on the floor...

They took me back into surgery and fixed me up. Apparently it's a pretty common thing when boys hit puberty. What happened to me is called torsion, and it's when the two nuts start twisting around each other inside the sack, and it eventually cuts off all the blood circulation. So they stitched each one of my balls to its correct side of my scrotum. They caught it just in time before I would've lost one, but after the test results came back, the doctor said I'd have less than a 1 percent chance of ever producing a child naturally.

Which, even at that young age, sucked so bad. I was adopted, and I was an only child, so even when I was little, I always said I would one day have a big family with lots of kids.

I still want that. I want four kids, just like your parents had. I'll either have to adopt, or do all the fertility shit my parents tried before they eventually adopted me.

From: Kayla Lanmon
December 9, 2006

Gross.

From: Kayla Lanmon
December 9, 2006

Totally just kidding. Dear God, I'm so glad I'm having a girl. Jeez, between the two of us, if we ever had a boy, he'd be fucked in the balls department. Mix your torsion with the fact the boys in my family seem to have one ball that doesn't like to drop, and he'd have some bad luck. My girl only has to worry about getting her mommy's itty bitty titties.

I felt her kick for the first time today. It was crazy. At first I thought it was just gas or something (so sexy) but it kept happening over and over. You can't feel it on the outside with your hand yet, but I could feel it inside. So cool. I'm starting to like the feeling of being pregnant now. After all the morning sickness went away and I was able to keep down some food, it hasn't been bad at all.

They call the second trimester the honeymoon trimester. It's after all the symptoms of the first, and before you get so big and uncomfortable during the third. The only bad thing is nothing freakin' fits me. ~Hey, maternity clothes makers! Skinny chicks get knocked-up too!~ I used the hair-tie trick for a while, where you loop the tie through the buttonhole and then hook it onto the button to keep your pants closed. Yeah, I'm getting way too big for that now. So I went to Motherhood Maternity at the mall, and I tried on jeans in their "Extra-Small". It looked like I was trying on a circus tent.

From the back, you can't even tell I'm pregnant. I'm just

as little as I've always been, only now I have this little soccer ball right in front. I'll take some pictures and show you.

From: Jason Robichaux
December 14, 2006

So how long are you going to keep working? Are you going to keep your job and just take maternity leave, or are you going to quit? Personally, I think you should quit. You said you only have the job so you feel useful, and you can't get more useful than being a good mommy and raising your girl.

I have an old friend who had a baby and became a stay at home mom, and she eventually started going a little crazy though. So maybe you could finish up your degree or something. I'm sure there's a bunch of the classes you need that you could just take online. I hate that you've given up your dream of becoming a writer. Your blog posts are so fun to read; I can only imagine what one of your books would be like.

I've refrained from reading the ones from when you lived here. I've opened them up a couple times, but ended up chickening out. I don't want to remember what an asshole I was to you. I mean, I should, I deserve it, but I already feel guilty enough. I don't want to relive that shit.

Anyways.

I busted my ass when I got to Canada the other day. I got off the plane all decked out in my Texas shit, Wranglers and my cowboy boots, and as soon as I stepped outside onto the ground, my feet shot out from under me and I landed right on my ass. Not fun.

From: Kayla Lanmon
December 18, 2006

I talked to Casey at work today. I warned her that I'd be quitting in a few months. I already can't stand up at work for my whole shift. I had to buy a cushioned fold-up chair and bring it to work, because my back and hips start hurting when I stand for too long. I'm not even that big yet. But the doctor said it's this stuff called relaxin in my system. It's what gets your pelvis to loosen and then open up to let the baby out. It sucks. It feels like my hip is going to pop out of joint. Casey was very understanding though, and made me promise I'd bring the baby to see her.

I'm thinking about taking a tour of FTCC. It's Fayetteville's community college. Before I moved to Texas, I had gone to Methodist College. It was a private college that cost an obscene amount of money. Back then, all I had ever heard was 'college is expensive,' always hearing things about student loans and stuff. So I thought the price of their courses were the norm. Turns out, the same College Algebra class I took there, I could have taken at Kingwood College or here at FTCC for a fourth of the cost. There should be a class in high school that teaches you that shit.

From: Jason Robichaux
December 20, 2006

All right, I'm jumping on the bandwagon, because I'm bored as fuck. I'm sending you one of these survey things that's always going around MySpace.

Facts
Name: Jason
Birthday: January 25
Star Sign: Aquarius
Height: 6'
Weight: 185
Shoe Size: 10W
Favorites
Favorite Color: Red
Favorite Singer: Serj Tankien
Favorite Movie: Boondock Saints
Favorite TV Show: Three Stooges
Favorite Play: Phantom of the Opera
Favorite Food: Meat
Dreams
Dream Vacation: Egypt
Dream Job: Billionaire Project Controls Manager
Dream Pet: Pharaoh Hound
Dream House: Plantation style
Celebrity Girl Crush: Keira Knightley
Celebrity Guy Crush: Jason Statham

From: Kayla Lanmon
December 20, 2006

Facts
Name: Kayla
Birthday: September 3
Star Sign: Virgo
Height: 5'6"
Weight: ummm....at the moment, 118, but normally 100 when I'm not knocked up!
Shoe Size: 7.5
Favorites
Favorite Color: Grey and Pink
Favorite Singer: Jared Leto
Favorite Movie: Father of the Bride 2
Favorite TV Show: Supernatural...and Grey's Anatomy, *even though it guts me.*
Favorite Play: Chicago
Favorite Food: Smithfield BBQ Sandwiches
Dreams
Dream Vacation: Paris
Dream Job: Author
Dream Pet: A llama
Dream House: Plantation style, with a giant wraparound porch
Celebrity Girl Crush: Angelina Jolie
Celebrity Guy Crush: Jensen Ackles

Kayla's Chick Rant & Book Blog
January 5, 2007

I'm shaking. Absolutely about to come unglued. All the plans are in place. Today at work, I told Casey I'd need the week of January 25th off.
Jason
Is
Coming
To
Visit
Me.

Holy shit. Holy mothereffing SHIT! Okay, I'm getting ahead of myself. I'm sorry I haven't been posting as much lately. I've been spending so much time messaging back and forth with Jason and talking to him on the phone all the time that my blog posts have been slacking. But can you blame a girl?

For Christmas, I got an unexpected package on my doorstep, along with the best note ever. It was a basket overflowing with relaxation products. There were bath bombs, lavender-scented lotion and body wash, a massage rolly-tool thingy, and even a fluffy pair of purple slippers. And now that I think about it, that MySpace questionnaire Jason sent me makes a lot more sense now.

The note read, "For my favorite girl in the world. Hope this makes you feel as beautiful as you are. Love, Jason."

It had been perfect timing. I'd been feeling gross lately. None of my old clothes are fitting anymore, but I'm still too small to wear actual maternity clothes, so I just resorted to wearing sweats all the time.

After thanking him profusely over the phone, that's when he dropped a bomb on me. He was going to have a week off for his birthday while he was working up in Canada, and he wanted to fly down to visit me. I didn't take him seriously at first. I mean, why would he want to come visit a five-months-pregnant girl he used to bang? But he was for real, even had me send him names of close-by hotels so he could book one.

I'm so freaking excited I don't know what to do with myself!

What will it be like seeing him for the first time in a year and a half?

What will it be like seeing him while I'm pregnant?

Oh, and what will it be like seeing him when I'm married to another man?

Our conversations have a different tone now. It's more than a friendship, but not quite romantic. It's somewhere in between. I don't question it. I take what I can get when it comes to Jason. Anything is better than nothing at all. When

I went all those months without talking to him before, it was like I wasn't living; I was just surviving. And then the moment he called me for Thanksgiving, it's like he breathed life back into me.

I feel like my old self again...only pregnant.

Even my mom and granny have noticed a change in my demeanor. I let them chalk it up to the second trimester being good to me. Anni, however, wasn't buying it, and I ended up confessing everything to her. She didn't know I had talked to Jason at all since the time she was dyeing my hair in her kitchen, when he drunk dialed me. So I had a lot of catching her up to do. Needless to say, she wasn't very happy about the situation.

On the one hand, she very much dislikes Aiden. No amount of bribery on his part could change the fact she just doesn't care for him in the slightest, and she has no qualms about making that known, to everyone, including Aiden. But on the other hand, she also doesn't think it was right to be talking to Jason while I'm married to another man. I could try to feed her any line of bullshit I wanted about us being just friends, but she wasn't eating it. That's the one bad thing about having a best friend who knows you so well, I guess.

She knows my true feelings for Jason. She knows I'd drop everything in a heartbeat if he were to tell me he wants to be with me. Maybe that's sad...desperate...but what else could I do when I know in my very soul he's the one I'm meant to be with?

From: Kayla Lanmon
January 8, 2007

Oh, my gosh, I have so much I want to show you when you get here! It's mostly food. Okay, it's like, all food. But you have to understand, that's all there is in Fayetteville. Restaurants, a mall, a few movie theatres, and a shitload of car dealerships. But I have to show you what real BBQ is. And I'll take you to Chason's Grandsons. When I was little, it was just called Chason's, but the original restaurant burned down. They reopened it though, with all the old recipes of southern home cookin'. There's no way you won't love it. I've been eating there at least once a week since I got my appetite back.

When you get here, I'll tell you about the name I picked out for my daughter. I hope you like it.

Chapter Sixteen

Am I breathing? My strength fails me. Your picture, a bitter memory

Kayla's Chick Rant & Book Blog
Blog Post 1/23/2007

I'm a happy person, damn it! I'm happy sober; I'm a happy drunk, and I smile until my cheeks hurt. I'm so freakin' perky all the time. I always get invited to everyone's parties; I never get scrolled over when people are looking through their phones to see what's going on. Everyone loves for me to be around because I bring no drama. I'm shameless, and will make a fool of myself to make everyone laugh. I don't say these things to be conceited; I say it to show you how unlike me it is when I tell you...

I cried myself to sleep again last night. I cradled my swollen belly in my hands and rocked myself back and forth praying in a whisper, "Please, God, make him love me. I know you put us here to be together. Just make him realize it. Please!" The last word came out on a sob. I swear I'm not a horrible person, as I laid there crying over another man while I'm six months pregnant with my husband's baby.

I will never say what happened was a mistake. I believe everything happens for a reason. I also believe in soul mates. But what if one person finds their soul mate and the other one just refuses to acknowledge it? Can you be happy with anyone else? Or if once your soul finds its other half, are you doomed to long for them?

These are all questions I've asked myself since I left Texas a year and a half ago, since I left the man I know I'm supposed to share my life with. No, I didn't leave him. He told me to go. He told me there was no reason for me to stay since my semester of school ended. That's when happy, perky, shameless Kayla snapped.

The first time.

The second time I lost myself was the week of Jason's twenty-third birthday, on the day I couldn't deny any longer that he really wasn't coming to see me. I had held out, thinking maybe it was a trick. Maybe he was trying to surprise me by just showing up at my doorstep.

He'd told me he booked his flight...his hotel... everything. He had my home address. That had to be it, right?

That's why I hadn't heard from him in the past two

weeks, right?

Not a single phone call.

Not a single message.

Nothing.

His phone went unanswered, most of the time going straight to voicemail.

He was in Canada. Maybe he had to turn his phone off because it was too expensive to call internationally.

Maybe he lost Internet access. Was there a big snowstorm where he was up there?

No, that wasn't it. Because I could see his new pictures and stuff he'd post on MySpace. Which meant nothing had happened to him.

It's now a couple days after he was supposed to come. No surprise arrival. No reservation under that name at the hotel he said he was staying at. Not even a response to the happy early birthday message I'd sent him through tear-filled eyes on MySpace. It could only mean one thing.

He was disappearing from my life yet again.

Taking the breath he'd given back to me with him..

March 20, 2007

Oh, third trimester. You will be the death of me.

As I sit in the middle of my parents' living room on the hardwood floor next to Granny's feet, I toss another few peas into the bucket and throw away the hull. We've been shelling butter beans and peas for the past hour as I watch a rerun of *Grey's Anatomy*.

I'd made sure to fair-warn Granny that tonight I had to watch it, interrupting her constant view of QVC, because this was the only episode I've ever missed of my favorite show. I watch it religiously, and I had been absolutely devastated when the power had gone out during a thunderstorm, making me miss my weekly fix of the doctor soap opera when it originally aired.

"Into You Like a Train," the episode from season two, might send me into labor. Which I wouldn't complain about one bit. I sit Indian-style, riveted to the screen, completely forgetting about the peas in my hand until Granny lightly nudges my thigh with her toe to get me back on track. I am the one, after all, who begged her for a bowl of her butter beans and peas and some rutabagas with pork. Nothing, and I mean absolutely nothing in this world, is better than my granny's southern cooking.

On TV, there is an old man and a young woman on a table in the hospital who have just been through a train accident. They have a huge metal pole that has impaled both of them, skewering them together. One wrong move, and either one of them could bleed out. There is a severely risky surgery they have to undergo in order to remove the pole.

The young woman is engaged to be married, and even in excruciating pain, you can't help but fall for her sweet personality. When it is determined that only one of them will live because of the angle of the pole, which will have to be slid out to be removed, the old man wants to give his life in order to save hers, saying he had already lived a long, fulfilling life, when she still has her whole journey ahead of her. She wants to wait to have the surgery until her fiancé arrives at the hospital, but there isn't enough time.

And then it happens. We discover the woman's injuries are more substantial than the old man's, and so she will be the one moved off the pole first, with the promise they will do everything they can to save both of the passengers. But as soon as she's off the metal tube, she crashes. After a short period of them trying to save her, all the attention is turned to the old man, who has more of a chance of living.

And I lose it.

With Meredith screaming, "What about her? We can't just abandon her!" I crush the peas in my fists and bawl as I watch the drama unfold.

"KD, you better calm down. You're gonna get yourself too upset and send yourself into labor," Granny scolds, tossing more shelled peas into the bucket.

"It's just so *sad!* He was giving up his life so she could live, and then she dies! They don't have enough doctors to work on both of them, so they just give up on her," I sniffle out.

"It's just a TV show, baby. It ain't real," she tries to soothe me.

"It's not just a TV show, Granny. They're my *friends*!" I wail.

I hear my mom burst out laughing from the couch on the other side of me, and I turn a death glare on her with my tear-filled eyes. "Oh, my poor little doll. May fifth can't get here soon enough. You need to have that baby so you'll have less time on your hands to obsess over fictional characters," she says, leaning forward and reaching out to rub my back.

"I've spent every single week with these people for the past three years," I explain.

"I get it, KD. Granny and I have watched our stories every day since the seventies. You don't have to try to get me to understand feeling like these people are real," Mom tells me, referring to *The Young and the Restless* and *The Bold and the Beautiful.*

"Well, Aiden comes home next week, and you'll be busy with him. No more moping around here like your puppy died," Granny orders.

The thought only depresses me more.

They don't know the reason the episode really hit home is because Dr. Derek Shepard just left Meredith for his cheating estranged wife, essentially abandoning her, the way I feel Jason abandoned me. It's been over two months, and I still haven't heard anything from him. No explanation of why he didn't come to see me, or even one for just falling completely off the grid. He hasn't even been updating his MySpace, so I have no way of knowing if he's okay.

Now, Aiden will soon be home, and I'll have to put up with his shit. I've gotten so used to doing things my way, doing whatever the hell I want, when I want. No one telling me I *can't* do something. This deployment has been way better than the last one, in the fact I talk to him maybe once a week, and he doesn't seem to give a crap what I'm up to. No more psycho controlling asshole this time.

The conversations are usually short and to the point. He asks me how I'm feeling and how the baby is doing. He calls when he knows I've had a doctor's appointment, and sometimes when he's just bored. Maybe he thinks he has nothing to worry about since I'm huge and pregnant. But in all actuality, I've gotten more compliments and flirtatious looks from gorgeous soldiers than I ever did before.

Even though I feel like absolute hell, with my sore hips and aching back, insomnia, and acid reflux like a motherfucker, I also have never felt more beautiful. I have a soft look about me now. No more boniness. My breasts are full and heavy, my hips are rounded, and I have an ass for days. My thighs even touch! Barely, but still. I wish I could keep all this extra meat on my bones after Josalyn arrives. But if I'm anything like my mom, I'll walk out of the hospital back in my skinny jeans.

Having this belly brings out the best in other people, I've discovered. I can't remember the last time I had to open a door for myself, or had to carry anything heavy. I can't go out into public without someone complimenting me on how "adorable" my baby bump is. Sure, it's also brought out people's annoying side too—unwanted advice, unwanted touches to my belly, unwanted birthing horror stories—but all in all, it's been nice. If it weren't for the physical aches and pains, I'd probably have a million kids.

Well, I say that now. Ask me again after I have her.

Kayla's Chick Rant & Book Blog
April 2, 2007

Aiden and I went to Womack today to take the tour of Labor & Delivery and a birthing class. That was...interesting. Looking around at all the other couples, you could see the love they had for one another, the excitement in the fathers' eyes when they helped their wives practice breathing techniques, the gentleness in their touches when helping them keep their balance on the exercise balls when we were learning different ways to ease labor pains.

I did my best to shake off the uneasy feeling inside me, making an effort not to flinch when Aiden's hands would touch me.

At the end of the class, I decided I wanted to make an appointment with the doula, learning during the two-hour course that a doula is a birthing coach, or companion. She explained she's there from the very first labor pains, through the entire birth, and even there afterwards to help with learning to breastfeed. I truly feel like I'll need her. Sure, I'll have my mom there, and my granny, but the way I feel about Aiden, I won't be like most women with husbands there for the delivery. I won't want to depend on him for support. I'd rather pay a doula, who I know will be there for me, because it's her job, and from talking with her, I can tell it's a job she absolutely loves.

I didn't hesitate for a second. I paid the woman and booked her as my labor companion. I want to have my baby as naturally as possible. I'm not against the drugs, but I want to see if I can physically do it myself, see how strong I can be. I've always been seen as this weak little fragile thing. How badass would I feel about myself if I could give birth naturally? Pretty damn badass. So that's my birth plan!

Hospital tour—check.

Labor class—check.

Doula—check.

Hospital bag packed—check.

All that's left now is to have my baby shower and then wait for little Josalyn to make her big debut!

CHAPTER Seventeen

Sleep brings release, and the hope of a new day

April 29, 2007

Not two weeks after Aiden got home from deployment, he got the news he'd be going back soon after I have Josalyn. They will soon be closing Pope Air Force Base, turning it into an Army airfield, and have been relocating a bunch of the airmen. We requested we stay here in Fayetteville as long as possible, since my family is here, instead of being one of the families to leave as soon as possible. Seems like most everyone jumped at the opportunity to get out of Fayettenam, so they seemed grateful we wanted to stay.

With the low number of airmen at the base now, though, that means the turnaround time for deployments is much quicker than before. I'm not complaining. Since Aiden's been back, I already broke one of his Playstation remotes, and cussed him out on several occasions. Nothing had changed since before he deployed—hell, since before I got pregnant. If anything, it's gotten even worse. Looking at us together, you'd never be able to tell we are a couple, much less married with a baby on the way. We look more like two strangers tolerating each other's existence.

My baby shower was a couple weeks ago. A bunch of my old friends from high school came, like the beautiful Katie and Barbara, who bought me the most adorable outfits for the baby, along with Brittany, and Anni of course. I became good friends with Sara, the girl I trained at work to replace me, and she made Josalyn the most amazing quilt, plus the cutest diaper bag for me, by hand. But who has turned out to be my lifesaver? My friend since freshman year, Katrina. Oh, thank the heavens for Katrina.

I've been having back spasms for a couple of days now, and absolutely nothing has been helping. Katrina, who used to give back rubs in class when the teachers weren't watching, went on to become a massage therapist. And Lord, are her hands magical. At first, she gave me a gift certificate for a massage at her work, and I promptly used that at her next available time slot. But when I told her about my back spasms, she actually came to my house.

Aiden took me up to Womack the day before yesterday, and they hooked me up to all the machines and saw I was having small contractions. They called them Braxton Hicks. It didn't seem right to me, because from all the reading I'd done, Braxton Hicks aren't supposed to come at regular intervals lasting all day. But whatever, there's nothing I can do about it, because the policy at the hospital is they can't admit me until I'm four centimeters. I've been at one centimeter since my last doctor's appointment. So they sent me home with 800mg Motrin, the military's solution to everything.

Then yesterday, the pain still wasn't lessening, so we went back to the hospital. This time, they sent me home with Percocet, telling me to come back only when I go into actual labor. How they think I'd be able to tell the difference between this pain and 'actual labor,' I have no idea.

Today, though, the back spasms are tremendously worse, and I called Katrina to see if she had a time slot open for a massage appointment. Being the sweetheart she is, she said she'd make a house call, since it's her day off from work. And so here I lie, in my sports bra and pajama shorts on my bed with my body pillow between my legs and under my belly, as Katrina works her magic on my lower back.

Aiden has been trying to call Susan, my doula, for an hour to see if she has any recommendations to help ease the pain in my back, so when the phone rings, he snatches it up immediately when he sees her name on the screen, putting the call on speaker so I can hear from the bed. She apologizes for not answering right away. Another one of her clients is in labor. Aiden explains what's going on, and tells her what the hospital told us. She also thinks the Braxton Hicks thing isn't right, and she tells us she'll do some digging and call us back.

After about an hour, Katrina leaves, telling me if I

need her, not to hesitate to call. In the two hours she's been here, I've felt more taken care of than I have in the past year. What a wonderful, selfless friend.

But only a short time later, the eased pain is back, and it's a hundred times worse. I know these aren't just 'practice contractions.' Maybe in the beginning, two days ago, it was my body preparing to go into labor, but since then, they have been coming more and more frequently, and getting stronger and stronger. Each time it happens, I can feel the muscles of my stomach squeezing tightly, taking my breath away. I try to use the techniques they taught us in the class, but it's so painful I can't catch my breath.

Soon, I'm in so much pain I'm screaming through each contraction, which I know for a fact is what these are, no matter what the asshats at Womack say. My mom holds one of my hands in hers and rubs my back with the other as she sits next to me on the edge of my bed, my head resting on her shoulder as I cry out my agony. I've held off calling Susan, because I know her other client is in labor, but thankfully, before we even try to contact her, Susan calls us and tells us to go to the hospital. According to what I've told her, she thinks I've actually been in labor for two days now, but she has a feeling there's something wrong with my cervix.

When we get there, I'm greeted in Labor & Delivery by a beautiful, petite, and curvy brunette. I don't know how I notice what she looks like through my torment, maybe because I've felt like I look like crap for the past few months, but she looks anxious to get her hands on me. When she approaches, she asks quietly if I'm Susan's girl Kayla, and I nod vigorously.

"Come on," she says, taking my arm. "I've got you a bed saved in here. If what is happening is what I think is happening, things are going to start moving fast. But don't worry. I always take care of Susan's girls."

Aiden stays behind at the station to fill out some paperwork as the nurse, who tells me her name is Jamie, leads me through a door and then into a curtained-off section containing a bed and a few machines. Just as I go to hike my butt up on the bed, another contraction hits, and I double over. Jamie wraps her arm underneath me, across my collarbone, to help hold me up, and instructs me to match her breath as she pants. Surprisingly, concentrating on matching her works a lot better than trying to use the breathing techniques by myself, and soon the pain fades and she assists me as I get up on the bed.

Once I'm settled, she hooks up a blood pressure cuff to my arm and wraps two Velcro belts around my belly that have monitors hooked to them. She adjusts them, explaining one is to track the baby's heartbeat to make sure she's not under too much stress, and the other is to track my contractions. When another one hits a few minutes later, Jamie pulls the scrolling paper up to look at the squiggly lines, and then looks up at me with wide eyes.

"How long have you been like this?" she asks, visibly trying to keep her voice calm.

"Um...it started two days ago, but got really bad early this morning," I explain, glancing at the giant round clock on the wall and seeing it's now four in the evening. "I've come to the hospital every day, and they just kept sending me home saying they were Braxton Hicks, and they couldn't admit me until I'm four centimeters."

"Has anyone checked your cervix?" she asks, moving to a drawer and pulling out a tube of lubricant.

"Not since the first day I came. They said I was still at a one." Feeling her anxiety, I wonder what is going on. What is it she thinks is going on? "Is everything okay? Is my baby all right?"

"Your baby is doing great. It's you I'm worried about. I'm going to check your cervix and see if you've dilated anymore. According to the readings, you should be at a seven," she says quickly, pulling up stirrups for me to place my ankles in.

It's my turn for my eyes to go wide. We learned in the birthing class that with each centimeter, the contractions get stronger and stronger, and once you hit a six, that's when they get to the highest level of pain. If the machine is reading my contractions are that strong, saying I should be dilated a seven, it's no wonder I'm in so much agony.

"Exactly what I thought," the nurse breathes. "I feel scar tissue on your cervix. Have you ever had a terminated pregnancy? It says this is your first one on your chart," she asks, her brows furrowed.

"No, this is my very first pregnancy," I state.

"Can you think of anything that could cause trauma to your cervix?" she asks, clearly trying to think of other reasons there could be scar tissue there.

"No. The only thing I can think of is at the beginning

of my pregnancy, my pap smear came back abnormal, and I had to do a colposcopy. I had yelled out in pain it had hurt so bad, but the doctor told me it only hurt that bad because of the extra blood flow down there from being pregnant," I explain, talking about the biopsy they did on my cervix when I was about eight weeks along.

"The doctor was wrong. You should barely feel a colposcopy because there are hardly any nerves in your cervix. I'll look into it later and find out who that butcher was, but right now, I've got to fix what that asshole screwed up," Jamie tells me. She pats my thigh, indicating to come out of the stirrups, then grasps my hand to help me sit up in the bed as she steps on the pedal on the floor that moves the back up into a seated position. "I'll be right back. I have to go get a few things."

As she hurries away, Aiden walks in through the curtains. He looks anxious, with his hands in his pockets and stiff posture. I don't have time to say anything to him before another contraction hits, and I crumple the paper sheet in my fists as I try to pant my way through it.

Aiden comes up next to the bed and takes my hand in his. I concentrate on trying to crush the bones in his hand, and soon, the pain subsides. I let go of his hand and internally smirk as I see him flex his fingers.

"What did the nurse say?" he asks, taking a seat in the chair next to the bed.

"The colposcopy I had while you were deployed caused scar tissue to form across my cervix. It basically sewed me shut. I'm not really sure what she's going to do, but she ran out of here to go gather supplies," I tell him.

I can't help it. I've tried to be so strong through this whole thing, but sitting in the awkward quiet of the hospital room with Aiden suddenly gets to me, and my chin trembles. I stave it off as long as I can, but I'm so exhausted, only having been able to sleep a couple hours in the last three days while the Percocet had worked its magic, the dam finally bursts.

Aiden jumps out of the seat and rushes to me, pulling me into his arms. It's a weird feeling, both hating his touch but at the same time needing to be held. I make a decision to pick my battles today, and give in to the comfort his arms provide. I soak the front of his shirt with my tears, and I cry into his chest, "I can't have a C-section. Didn't you hear the horror stories your friends told us about C-sections at a military hospital? They'll butcher me. Just like what the nurse said the doctor did to my cervix. They can't cut me open! I even wrote in my birth plan I don't want an episiotomy. Susan said if the baby is too big, then I should just tear naturally, and I'll only tear as much as she needs to get through. If they cut me, the healing would take a lot longer. I wanted her to come naturally. I wasn't even going to get an epidural, but I don't think I can take this much longer. It hurts so b-bad."

I continue to bawl into his chest as he rubs my back, rambling on and on about what I had wanted, how I had planned for my daughter to come into the world. It was going to be peaceful, with my wonderful doula there to hold my hand and guide me through it. I was supposed to transition into different positions while using specific breathing techniques to help move the baby along until she would finally come into the world and be immediately placed on my chest.

But instead, I'm here with a husband who I feel is only here out of obligation, after being in labor for three days with no help even from the hospital, waiting for the nurse to come back with God only knows what kind of supplies she's going to have to use to 'fix' what the doctor had done to me. So, I let myself cry until Aiden rocks me into a stupor.

When Jamie comes back, she's not alone. The other nurse introduces herself as Heather, and she tells me she is going to hook me up to an IV to get some fluids in me.

"Once she does that, we're going to move you into your L&D room," Jamie says, and then to distract me from the needle about to go into my arm, she explains what is to come. "I know you are in excruciating pain—"

God has perfect comedic timing, because at that exact moment, the strongest contraction yet hits, and both she and Aiden hold my hands as I pant and cry my way through it.

Jamie continues her explanation when the tightening releases. "This is called a Foley balloon." She holds up what looks like a small, clear whoopee cushion attached to a tube. "What we're going to do is roll this up really small and put it in the opening of your cervix. Then we'll fill it with water very slowly, and as it fills, it'll break apart that scar tissue that's holding you closed."

"Oh, my God, that sounds painful," I breathe.

"You won't even feel it. As soon as we get you moved,

the anesthesiologist is going to come and give you an epidural. After the balloon does its job, we'll hit you with some Pitocin to get your cervix caught up in centimeters with your contractions," she informs me, undoing the Velcro belts from around me.

"Oh, God. Pitocin? They told us about that in the class. That shit sounds like devil jizz," I blurt. Jamie and Heather laugh as Aiden helps me stand and then move to sit in the wheelchair that's waiting for me at the foot of the bed.

"If you're going au naturel, then yes, devil jizz is the perfect description for it. Makes you feel like there is a demon inside you trying to break out. But since you're having an epidural first, you won't even tell the difference."

Jamie takes hold of the wheelchair's handles behind me as Heather walks beside us pushing the rolling metal stand holding the bag of IV fluid. At the end of the hall, we wait for the elevator to arrive, and then they roll me in, the four of us not talking, as if we're all waiting for the next contraction to hit. Surprisingly, we make it into the private delivery room without one coming.

Soon after I'm settled in the bed with all the monitors reattached to my belly and arm, the anesthesiologist comes in. He's young, with a dark high-and-tight haircut and pristine scrubs, very handsome. His youth doesn't bother me at all, because this...this is the bringer of the drugs. By now, I couldn't give two shits about having my baby without medication. Nope, I'm ready to drop to my knees and do terrible things to the doctor if he'll just give me the damn drugs.

He glances at the chart and then slides it into the plastic holder on the wall. "Mrs. Lanmon, I'm Dr. Williams. I'll be giving you your epidural. I know from your birth plan you didn't want one, but I think circumstances have changed your mind. Am I right?"

"Dear Lord, please just give it to me," I half-growl, surprising everyone, including myself.

Dr. Williams chuckles then instructs me on what to do. "Alrighty then. You're going to sit up at the side of the bed and drape yourself over either the nurse or your husband, hunching over as far as your belly will let you. You'll take a deep breath, and as you let it out, I'll insert the epidural into your lower back. You have to be very still when I do it. Don't jump, and try your hardest not to even flinch. One wrong move and the medicine won't work. Or maybe it'll only numb one side. You don't want that to happen."

"Okay, so roll into a ball and don't move. Got it. No problem, now give it to me!" I say, leveraging myself up.

Jamie rushes forward to help me as Aiden stands at the side of the bed. I don't care who it is I drape myself over. Aiden's there already, so he's going to be my leaning post, since that'll get me the epidural fastest.

I feel the doctor work as he explains everything he's doing, prepping the area with alcohol where he's going to insert the needle. And as luck would have it, God and his sense of humor strike again, sending me into a contraction of epic proportions as Aiden instinctively wraps his arms tightly around me, holding me still as the doctor inserts the needle.

The good thing about the timing of the contraction is I

don't even feel it when the epidural goes in, and when it wanes off as Dr. Williams tapes everything in place, I lie back on the bed, deliriously exhausted. A few minutes later, I feel my stomach tighten, but there is no pain.

Jamie smiles. "Look at the monitor. See? There is your contraction, but it doesn't hurt, right?"

I watch as the neon green line on the black screen spikes high above the bottom line, and then I turn back to her and grin. "Thank you, sweet baby Dr. Jesus."

The last thing I remember is everyone in the room bursting out laughing as I finally drift off into blissful sleep.

CHAPTER Eighteen

It sounds so sweet, coming from the lips of an angel

"They're waking her up now," I hear Aiden say, and I crack one eye open to see he's on the phone. "Yeah, they're going to do the balloon and give her Pitocin, and then you can head up here." After a pause, he replies, "No, we don't need anything. The hospital bag was already in the car. She's not allowed to eat or drink anything except ice chips until the baby comes. One sec, Ava, she's coming out of it."

I lift my head to see Jamie carefully rolling the Foley balloon until it's about the size of a cigarette. I look to my right and see Heather rubbing my arm, and everything suddenly clicks into place, where I am, what's happening, and who it is on the phone.

"We let you sleep for a couple of hours, but we didn't

want to wait any longer to get things moving. Susan told me on the phone you hadn't gotten any sleep in the last couple of days, and I thought it was important to get you a little rest to have strength to get this sweet baby out," Jamie tells me.

All I can do is nod in my stupor, and I listen as Aiden tells my mom, "They're putting it in. Now she's got a big-ass syringe and is filling it, pushing water into the tube... She's good. She looks like she's falling back to sleep."

With that announcement, I feel Heather rub my arm again, bringing me back. I don't know why I have to be awake for this, but since it seems so important to them, I concentrate on staying conscious.

"There we go. It worked," Jamie says with a bright smile. She uses the syringe to suck the water back out of the balloon then sits it on the metal rolling tray beside her. She gives a little tug on the tube to remove the balloon, and when she does, I feel a huge release inside me, and all of a sudden the bed beneath me is very, very warm.

I look up at Aiden confused as he stops explaining what the nurse is doing midsentence. I watch half amused, half concerned as he wobbles on his feet, his face turning ghostly pale. "Is she okay?" he finally whispers to the room.

Jamie gives a short laugh. "Oh, yeah. She's great. Her water just broke. Won't be long now."

After he revives some of his color, he speaks into the phone, "Her water broke. I've never seen anything like it. I...I gotta go, Ava. You coming up here soon?" A pause. "Okay, see you in a few." And he shuts his phone.

Relief fills me knowing my mom will be here in a little

while, and I'm sure she'll be bringing Granny with her. That was my number one wish in my birth plan. I couldn't care less if Aiden was here, but I wanted my mom and granny to be here. Granny was the nurse when I was born, and I thought it would be amazing to have her here with me for the delivery of our little princess. If I can at least have that one thing go right, then I will be happy.

A woman in dark scrubs and a white coat comes into the room after knocking lightly on the door, and when she approaches the bed, she reaches out her hand and shakes mine. "Hi, Kayla. I'm Dr. Snowdon. I'll be delivering your baby."

"Nice to meet you," I reply. Being a military hospital, you don't see the same doctor at every appointment or get to pick who is there to deliver your baby. It's whoever is on duty that day. The woman is very pleasant though, soft spoken, and she immediately puts me at ease.

"Nurse Vest has caught me up on all your adventures with your little one the past couple of days," she informs me, nodding at Jamie. "So why don't we kick this thing up a notch and add some Pitocin? The baby is doing great, no worries there, but since your body has been going through this for such an extended period of time, we don't want to take any chances."

"Sounds good to me." I shrug.

"All right. We'll add that to your IV, and then you can try to get some more rest while you can. She winks at me and then nods at Heather, who disappears behind me, I'm assuming to add the meds to my tubes. I'm beginning to feel like a science experiment, but if all of it gets me through this with a healthy baby girl in my arms at the end, then I'll be a guinea pig all they want.

A short time later, when I'm starting to doze off, there is a quiet knock on the door, and I could cry I'm so happy when it opens and in walks my mom and granny. Suddenly, everything is right in my world. I feel an overwhelming strength fill my entire body just at the sight of the most important women in my life. If it was time, I feel like I could push Josalyn out in one try. My face splits into a huge grin as Mom hurries over to me and Granny shuffles along behind her. They both wrap me in a hug, being careful not to hit the IV attached to my wrist.

When they pull back, Mom takes one look at me and gets to work. She gently pulls my hair out of it's messy, tangled knot on my head and works her fingers through it, pulling it back into a bun that keeps it all blissfully out of my face. She pulls out a pack of gum from her pocket and hands me a stick of the minty goodness, and my mouth immediately feels ten times better. She hands Aiden the empty cup on the rolling table next to me and instructs him to go fill it with ice chips in a way that scolds him for even letting it get low. All the while, Granny is walking around the bed and making sure I'm all nice and tucked in.

Jamie comes in, and seeing the newcomers, she introduces herself and then updates everyone on what's been going on. She also tells me Susan called her, saying to tell me she is so very sorry she has to miss the birth. We knew it was possible for this to happen. I'm in labor a full week before my due date, and Susan had told us if one of her clients went into labor before me, then we'd get a full refund for the $600 we paid her to be my doula. I was just grateful she pulled strings at the hospital and got the nurse to check for the scar tissue. That alone was worth the money to me. God only knows what could've happened if it had gone on any longer.

After eating a few ice chips, exhaustion wins out once again, and I feel myself drift off to sleep.

"KD...KD girl...wake up, doll." I hear as something tickles my face. For a second, I think I'm ten years old in my bed at home, my mom annoyingly feathering kisses all over my face to wake me up for school. I swat at the tickling on my nose, and I hear her laugh lightly. "KD...you gotta wake up, baby. You're ten centimeters. It's time to bring our little doll into the world, sweet girl."

That brings me out of it. I jerk all the way awake with a gasp, opening my eyes and seeing not my childhood bedroom with it's pretty cream wallpaper with tiny pink hearts, but my delivery room. The lights have been turned down low, but there is a bright lamp being set up at the foot of the bed. I see Jamie, Heather, and Dr. Snowdon prepping, putting on fresh gloves and tying masks around their faces.

I look off to my left and see Dr. Williams standing near the machine that controls the epidural and IV. My mom and granny are next to the bed, Mom stroking my hair, and Granny rubbing my thigh, which I see but can't feel. Aiden is to my right, looking nervous, not knowing what he should be doing.

I'm so out of it I have no idea how much time has passed since arriving at the hospital, so I look up at Mom and ask, "What day is it?"

She smiles at me again, answering, "It's Monday, baby. April thirtieth." She turns around to look at the clock on the back wall. "It's about 3:30 in the afternoon."

"My girl wanted diamonds," I say tiredly.

"What?" She chuckles, probably thinking I'm talking through a stupor.

"Her due date was May fifth, which would have been emeralds as her birthstone. She's coming out early, but very last minute, just in time to have diamonds," I explain with a sleepy grin.

"Ah, sapphires and diamonds. What a pretty mother's ring you'll have," Granny says, and the three of us laugh, knowing Granny loves any excuse to buy jewelry off QVC.

Jamie comes up to the head of the bed and starts raising it using the remote. "All right. We're going to sit you up, and then someone needs to hold each of your legs. When we see a contraction coming on the screen, Dr. Snowdon will tell you to push, and you push as hard as you can for ten seconds. I know you can't feel what's going on down there, but if you just focus on pushing down and out, you'll be doing exactly what you need."

My heart starts pounding rapidly, and all of a sudden, I get very scared. I grab Granny's hand on my thigh and look up into my mom's eyes, and I know she can see the fear there, because her face goes soft. She leans down right in my face, her beautiful blue eyes boring into my green ones, and she says low but clear, "You can do this, baby. We're right here, and we're going to help you. All you have to do is push. And then we'll get to hold our girl."

I take a deep breath and then nod vigorously, drawing on the strength I hear in Mom's voice and feel in Granny's grip on my hand. I look over at Jamie and tell her, "Okay, I'm ready," and before I can even prepare myself, Dr. Snowdon says, "Perfect timing, because here comes your contraction. Positions, everyone."

Mom and Granny take ahold of my left leg, and Aiden grabs the other, their grips on the backs of my thighs, my heels pressing into their opposite palms, and when the doctor says, "Deep breath...and push! Ten...nine..." and continues to count, everyone counts along with her, and I push with all the strength in my little body. If I have to do it this way, the only thing going right on my birth plan being my favorite two women in the world are here, then dammit, I'm going to do it right. No pussy-footing around. And I feel a little bit of pride in myself when the doctor reaches one, and tells the room, "There we go! Good girl! She's already crowning."

I see Granny peek over the sheet across my knees, and a grin splits her face. "She's got a headful of dark hair, KD. That's why you had all that heartburn!"

I cough out a laugh, catching my breath while I can before I have to push again. Holding my breath for ten seconds never felt so long before. Tears fill my eyes imagining what Granny is seeing.

What seems like only moments later, Dr. Snowdon says another contraction is coming, and we all tense for her signal. She repeats, "Deep breath…and push! Ten…nine…" and again, everyone in the room says the numbers excitedly, but I notice an annoying loudness to my right that makes me very angry, distracting me from the hard work I'm trying to do at the moment. When they get to one, I turn to Aiden with his impending death in my eyes, and say through my panting breaths, "If you do not stop screaming in my ear, I'm going to grab those umbilical cord scissors on that tray and cut your damn dick off."

I vaguely notice Heather guffaw behind Dr. Snowdon, but in this moment, I'm not embarrassed in the slightest. I'm dead serious. Aiden must see it in my glare, because he quickly apologizes, "I'm sorry, baby. I was just in the moment. It's so exciting. I'm sorry. It's just so intense! I'll quiet down, promise."

"Okay, let's make this one count. No yelling in Mom's ear, Dad," the doctor scolds teasingly. "Give me a really good one like the first one. All we gotta do is get her shoulders out, and it'll be a homerun."

My mom smooths some hair that has come loose from my bun out of my face and then leans forward to kiss my forehead. "You've got this, baby girl. You ready?"

"Yeah, Mommy. I'm ready to see her," I whisper.

"All right, here we go, folks!" Dr. Snowdon calls, and they begin the countdown once more, Aiden much more quiet this time. Instead of holding my breath this time, I growl out with all my strength, not caring about embarrassing myself, and when the doctor says quietly but clearly, "That's it…that's it," I feel the most overwhelming sense of relief I've ever felt before as I open my eyes and see her pull Josalyn all the way out and then up above the sheet across my legs.

I immediately burst into tears at the sight of her, my arms jutting out to welcome her as Dr. Snowdon stands and places her on my chest, exactly how I had dreamed. As I look down at Josalyn through the tears in my eyes, I barely notice as one nurse towels her off while the other suctions fluid out of her mouth. And that's when I hear her voice for the very first time. She gives one loud wail, and then it is nothing but sweet newborn baby noises.

At some point, Aiden cuts the umbilical cord. Maybe it was before she was even handed to me; I'm not sure, because my mind is so blown from both the birth of my daughter and from pure exhaustion.

The next few minutes, I'm in a daze. Everything going on around me is a blur. Josalyn is taken from me, but Aiden and Granny go with her to oversee her first bath. I'm confused when Jamie asks if I want to see my afterbirth. I must say yes in my stupor, even though I have no desire to see it, because she lifts the pan and shows me the most god-awful looking thing I've ever seen in my life. What has been seen cannot be unseen, and I'll have to remember that sight for the rest of my life.

I finally notice the doctor is still working between my legs behind the sheet, and I mumble, "Everything all right down there?"

"Oh, you're fine. Just a little tear, because you Hulk'ed her out of you," she jokes. "I'm just putting in a couple stitches. These will dissolve on their own, so you don't have to worry about coming to get them out."

"My first stitches," I murmur.

"Really, what about that scar on your chin there?" she inquires, nodding toward my face.

Mom jumps in to tell the story. "That scar is from when she was seven. It was the day of her dance recital she had been practicing all year for, and this one decided she was going to sneak up and scare me. There is a step down from the carpeted landing in our family room, down to the hardwood floor of the kitchen, and when she was creeping up on me on her hands and knees, her hand shot out from under her when she tried to go down that step. Landed right on her chin. Blood went absolutely everywhere. If we would've gone to the hospital to stitch her up, she would have missed her recital, so she begged us not to take her. Granny, being a nurse, was able to clean it up really good and then put butterfly bandages on it to keep it closed. In her recital picture, she has all those bandages on her chin, but the biggest toothless smile you've ever seen." She laughs, then finishes the story I've heard her tell a million times. "After the recital, we took her to the Emergency room, but they said it had already started to scab up; she didn't need stitches."

"So you've been a strong woman all your life," Dr. Snowdon states.

I don't know why, but what she said affects me. Maybe it's the drugs in my system, or the fact I've only had a few hours of sleep in the past four days, but when she makes that statement, it hits me right in the gut, right where I need it. I think about the past few days and realize, *Damn, I am a badass motherfucker.*

Three days. Three whole days I was in labor, the most painful thing in human existence, before I was given anything for the pain. And then after all that trauma, I 'Hulk-ed' my baby out in three pushes.

No matter how weak I may feel on the inside all the time, letting stupid men affect how I feel about myself, I realize what Dr. Snowdon told me is true. In that moment, I feel better than I've felt in two years, since the day I left Houston, which is really saying something, since I just went through childbirth.

CHAPTER Nineteen

Pain. So much fucking pain. Dare I say even more painful than labor, and a hell of a lot worse than delivery. When my epidural wears off, I can suddenly feel every single thing that happened to my poor little body over the weekend. And on top of all that, the small tear from pushing Josalyn out so fast feels more like I've been stabbed in the vagina with a machete. Sprinkle on a couple hemorrhoids, and I'm in absolute hell.

But...and yes there's a *big* but...combine all that excruciating agony, and not even it can compare to the torture that is breastfeeding.

Dear God, what about all those beautiful pictures of mothers blissfully breastfeeding their babies, a look of pure love and contentment on their faces? If someone were to take a picture of me right now, they'd see a woman being masochistically tortured. As Josalyn nurses away at my right breast, I wail at the ceiling through my suffering, tears streaming down my face, running down my neck, soaking the blanket she's wrapped in.

I no longer feel very strong.

When I look down at her though, all my motherly instincts go off, and I quiet my crying so I don't scare her. She looks so happy, her tiny little fist resting at my cleavage, her eyes at half-mast as she suckles away. I concentrate on how soft her skin is as I run my fingertip over her pink cheek, and it almost...*almost* makes the pain lessen.

I sent Aiden away a while ago. When he tried to comfort me when she first latched on, I went absolutely ape shit. I didn't want him near me, much less touching me, and I told him to go away and leave me the hell alone, and while he was at it, to tell the nurse to call the lactation consultant.

It's been almost exactly twenty-four hours since I had my girl, and I haven't been able to part with her except to let them run their tests, telling them to bring her back to me whenever they were done. Having her inside me for the past nine months, it felt strange, uncomfortable, to be away from her.

There's a light knock on my post-partum room door, which I got lucky and had my own. A cute brunette pops her head in, asking if it's okay to come in. I nod, wiping at my cheeks and nose. She hurries to my bedside table and grabs a couple of tissues, handing them to me. "Hey, sweetheart. I'm Erin, your new nurse on duty and lactation consultant."

"Oh, thank God," I breathe.

"Nursing not going so well, huh?" she asks, standing up on her tiptoes to look down at Josalyn. "She's got a very shallow latch. Take your thumb and press it on her chin to open her up, then shove more of your nipple in her mouth," she instructs.

I press my thumb to her chin, but nothing happens.

"Don't be scared. You aren't going to hurt her. Just push down with enough force to break the suction, and when her little mouth opens, lean forward and get as much of your areola in there as you can. It's hurting that bad because she's only sucking right on the tip, where all the nerve endings are," she explains.

Using a slightly more forceful hand, I get Josalyn's mouth to open wide, and then do what Erin said. Immediately, the pain lessens exponentially, and I breathe a sigh of relief. I look up at the nurse with a thankful smile.

"Girl, you look exhausted. How much sleep have you gotten since you had the little gremlin?" she asks.

"I sleep when she sleeps, so an hour or two here and there. But a lot of the time I just hold her and watch her sleep," I confess.

"You go home tomorrow. If you want my advice, let us take her to the nursery. We'll bring her to you when she needs to eat, but if you don't get some sleep, you're going to be miserable. Take advantage of us while you can. Trust me. You'll have plenty of time to watch her sleep when you go home."

She has a point. I feel slightly crazed. I could do with a good, long, uninterrupted sleep. I let out a heavy sigh and let my guilt release along with it. When I look down at my little girl again, I see she is sleeping, her mouth no longer suckling, so I lie her down between my legs on the bed and re-swaddle her in the blanket. I then lift the tiny bundle to my face and kiss that tissue-soft cheek before handing her to Erin.

"Oh, my goodness, what a cutie. She is gorgeous! A lot of babies are so tragic looking when they are first born, but this one? What a beauty," she coos, and my chest fills with pride. I did that. I grew that perfect little princess. "Do you need anything? It's close enough to the hour that I can give you your pain killers, that way I won't have to wake you up to give them to you."

"Oh, hell yes. Please. I never thought sitting up in bed could hurt so bad," I tell her.

"What's going on? You had her vaginally, yes?" she inquires.

"Yeah, but I tore a little, and every time I go from lying down to sitting up so I can go to the bathroom, I feel like I'm going to pass out from pain."

"All right. Let me take her to the nursery, and then when I bring your pills, I'll bring you my magic potion," she promises, and with that, she leaves the room, taking my baby girl with her.

I ease myself back from where I was slouching and look around the room. I don't know what to do with myself. I've gotten so used to having Josalyn inside me, always talking to her when no one else was around, that I feel utterly alone and empty. I try to enjoy the quiet, try to turn the feeling of loneliness into one of content solitude, but it doesn't work. So I sit there, wiggling my feet and tapping my fingers on the bed, antsy until Erin finally returns. But unfortunately, in walks Aiden right behind her.

Bless her heart, she has no idea what our relationship is like, and I can imagine any other couple would feel great about her doting, but it just makes me feel awkward. "Y'all made such a beautiful baby. What a proud daddy you must be! Your wife is a champ. Any husband with a woman who can survive all she went through is a lucky man."

She continues, not catching on to how uncomfortable her words are making the both of us, "Okay, so we're going to help your honey up and get her to the bathroom, and I'm going to teach both of you how to work this miracle foam."

"Ummmm..." I look between Erin and Aiden, not quite knowing what to say. I don't want him in there with me. God only knows what she's going to show us to do. The less he sees, the better. He's been helping me to the bathroom, but I've been doing everything else myself. When my mom was here, she helped me figure out the squirt bottle they wanted me to use instead of toilet paper, but after I got the hang of sitting on the toilet and turning on the sink to let the water warm up before filling the bottle, I've done it all myself each time. Which has been quite a lot, since they still have me on fluids through an IV. They took my catheter out right before my epidural wore off—thank goodness. That was something I did not want to feel.

"Oh, he got you into this," she says with a swat of her hand. "In sickness and in health, remember? It's his job to take care of you after you just gave birth to his baby."

There is nothing else she could have said that would've made me any less comfortable in this situation. But she doesn't know any better, so I can't really hold it against her. Normally, I would agree whole-heartedly with what she said, just not when it's applied to Aiden and me.

I switch gears in my head, telling myself I don't give a shit what he's about to see in the bathroom. I gave up trying to impress him a long time ago, so I'm not going to worry about grossing him out. I didn't ask him to come back; it's his own damn fault.

"So come around here, Dad, and let's get her out of bed. She said this is the worst part, so let's help her strain as little as possible," Erin instructs.

Aiden comes to the side of the bed I've swung my legs over. He places one of his arms around my lower back, and I wrap one arm around his shoulders, and grasp Erin's hand with my other, and with a deep breath, I force myself up. It still hurts terribly, but not as much as when I do it alone. Taking small, shuffling steps, the three of us move into the spacious bathroom.

Erin tells me to slide off what I've been calling my diaper, my granny-panties containing two giant maxi pads stuck side-by-side. I'm aware Aiden takes a step back as I pull them down, and even though I don't care what he thinks, a small part of me hopes he's not looking.

I peel off, roll up, and throw away the used pads, and then Erin instructs me to put in fresh ones. Before I pull them up though, she hands me a freshly filled squirt bottle of warm water, and has me clean myself off thoroughly.

"Okay, now this," she shows me what looks like a small can of hair mousse, "stuff is the shit. Right before you pull your undies up, squirt this all over the pads, and when you press the pads against you, it should be an instant relief."

I do exactly as she says, and when I pull them up, making sure not to waste any as I slide them up my legs, everything goes blessedly numb. I can't help it. I reach out and grab Erin in a tight hug, thanking her profusely. When I let go of her, she chuckles as she helps me back to bed.

I don't know when Aiden had left the bathroom, but he's now seated next to the bed in the chair that pulls out into a cot. He slept there last night. The only times I've let go of Josalyn have been to go to the bathroom and to nap while she was asleep. At those times, I handed her over to him to hold. I had a mix of emotions while seeing her in his arms. Part of me liked seeing it; there was nothing sweeter than seeing a man holding his brand new baby. But at the same time, I had this overwhelming sense of protectiveness, something telling me to not let my guard down. So I kept my momma-bear instinct strong, instead of telling it to chill out.

Erin helps me get settled in the bed once again, and this time sitting down doesn't shoot a stabbing pain through my nether regions. I take the pain pills she hands me with the bottle of water and then pull the covers over me as I lower the back end of the bed so I can lie down to sleep. "When you wake up, I'd take a shower if I were you. There's a seat in there for you to sit on, and the secret is to take one of the towels, fold it into a pad, and soak it with hot water before you sit down on it. Feels absolutely amazing," she says conspiratorially.

She pats me on my shoulder and then wishes Aiden and me good sleep before leaving the room. I'm asleep before the door even closes behind her.

Kayla's Chick Rant & Book Blog
May 10, 2007

Josalyn is a whole ten days old today! So much has happened since the day my lactation consultant-slash-nurse-slash-miracle worker taught me how to breastfeed correctly. And yet again, my mom was right.

After seeing me in so much pain while nursing the baby, she told me that on the fifth day, like magic, the pain would mysteriously disappear. She said it never failed; for some reason, day five was the exact day everything would just click into place, and breastfeeding would feel like the most natural thing in the world, which it was, and it did.

I wasn't allowed to leave the hospital until 3:55pm,

exactly 48-hours after Josalyn made her big debut. That morning, I had several visitors. Katie and Barbara came to see us, and so did Katrina. Before I could be released, I had to watch this awful and terrifying video on SIDS and Shaken Baby Syndrome, and was given a packet on post-partum depression.

I dressed my baby girl up in the precious powder pink going-home outfit Mom and Granny had picked out for her, and wrapped her up in the beautiful white baby blanket they'd given me at my baby shower. When I put her in her car seat the first time, she looked ridiculous, so teeny strapped down in the pink Graco carrier. I sat in the backseat with her, not willing to sit up front with her back there by herself.

When we got home, there was a welcome crew. Uncle Sam, Aunt Janie, Uncle Thurman, and Uncle Dan were all there, along with my dad, and of course Mom and Granny. Aiden carried Josalyn in while Mom took my hand, helped me up the front steps and inside, and then I had him sit her carrier on our giant kitchen counter. She made the most adorable centerpiece as all my relatives gathered around to get their first peek at the newest family member. My mom pulled me to the other side of the kitchen, where a beautiful bouquet of pink roses was displayed, a gift from her, Granny, and Dad.

The next day, Anni came to see us. I learned that soon after I had Josalyn, she had come to see us in the delivery room, but I have absolutely no memory of it. Being the thoughtful friend she is, she told me she saw how both overwhelmed and out of it I was, so she'd only stayed a few minutes, and waited a day to come to the house so I wouldn't be too frazzled by so many visitors. That, and she wanted Josalyn and me all to herself, which she knew she wouldn't get unless she let everyone else go first.

I also learned my Aunt Janie was one of the first people to see Josalyn too. She just so happened to be at the hospital with her mom and saw Granny and Mom when they first got there.

Since we knew Aiden was deploying not long after I was to have Josalyn, we didn't bother finding an apartment to move into with the baby. We decided it would be smarter to wait until he got back again, that way I'd have Mom and Granny close to help me with my newborn. Nine months pregnant, while Aiden sat on the bed playing his video games, I had built her brand new crib with my own two hands, making sure to put the base on the highest setting so it was more like a bassinet.

I followed all the rules in the wretched video, taking down the cute, colorful crib bumper and removing the stuffed animals to lessen the chances of SIDS. And since her very first visitor, no one has touched her without either thoroughly washing their hands or using hand sanitizer first. Oh yes, I was being one of those moms, a first time mother who wanted her baby to live in a bubble. I cringed when someone would kiss her face, but I also knew how excited everyone was about this little one, 'the baby's baby,' so I just bit my tongue.

She's so perfect. I remember a nightmare I'd had a couple months ago that she would be too good, never crying, and I forgot to feed and change her. She's very similar to the baby in that dream, but I never forget. Thank goodness for mother's instincts. That, and my boobs. Good Lord, if I go more than two hours without feeding her, I feel like these Pamela Anderson jugs are going to explode!

I'm ready for Aiden to deploy. I want to establish a routine. I'm tired of arguing with him. From the beginning, I've felt Josalyn is my baby, not his. He didn't really want a baby, just gave me what I wanted, basically to shut me up and get me off his back. So I've had no problem changing every diaper, giving her every bath, getting her to sleep every time, and, of course—since I'm not using bottles—feeding her every meal.

But when I caught him trying to get her to take a pacifier, after I made it perfectly clear I didn't want to use one since it can cause nipple confusion, making breastfeeding more difficult, I flipped out. She had started crying while I was taking a quick shower, distracting him from his online poker tournament, and instead of just picking her up and comforting her for a few minutes until I could get myself clean, he found a pacifier someone had given us at the baby shower. I walked in right as he was leaning over the crib, trying to get her to open her mouth with its tip.

I. Went. Apeshit. I don't care if he doesn't contribute to helping out with Josalyn. She's my responsibility. But purposely doing something I've specifically said not to do, just to get her to stop disturbing you, and then having the audacity to say, "I'm her dad. I can make the decision to give her a pacifier if I want," when you're not the one who feeds her every single meal, which you could potentially fuck up with that pacifier...you're just begging me to go Lorena Bobbitt on your ass.

I only have a couple more days to deal with him until he leaves. After the pacifier incident, I haven't left him alone with her. Granny and Mom have taken care of her anytime I needed to use the bathroom or shower, and if they weren't home, I strapped her into her carrier and took her in there with me.

I am going kinda stir-crazy though. Granny told me a newborn shouldn't go out into public until they're two weeks old, when their immunities are much stronger. So I haven't left the house since I came home from the hospital. It's the perfect excuse not to go to the hangar when Aiden deploys though. Not that he cares. I think he's as ready to leave as I am to have him go. He's already got everything packed up and loaded in his car, except for his beloved video games and laptop, of course. Those he'll wait until the very last second, since he'll probably play them up until the moment he walks out the door.

CHAPTER twenty

But that's just me trying to move on without you

June 13, 2007

    I signed up for the summer semester of school, deciding I could handle two classes for my first semester back. Josalyn's little body seems to be set on a timer, getting hungry and needing a diaper change at almost the exact same times every day. She even seems to have a set sleep pattern. She doesn't sleep through the night, but I've gotten into a groove with her.

    She goes to bed around 9 p.m., and sleeps until about two, when she wakes up for a little snack in the middle of the night. She easily goes back into her crib after I nurse her back to sleep. Then she awakens once again around five, and if I try to put her back in her crib that time, she won't go back to sleep. So I've learned if I nurse her in my bed, laying us front to front on our sides as she suckles, she falls asleep again. I unlatch her from my breast, and we're able to sleep a couple more hours.

She's such an easy baby, and so much fun. And Riley, he loves her to death. He's her little protector. He scooches up next to me while I'm feeding her, and if anyone tries to come near us, his hackles come up and the most godawful growl comes out of his tiny little four-pound body.

With the routine being so concise, I had a lots of downtime, so instead of being unproductive, I decided to start classes again. I'm taking a psychology and a computer class online. The psychology course is fascinating, and the computer course is easy, so I'm actually ahead on my assignments. I'm able to work at my own pace, and at this rate, I'll be finished way before the semester is over.

I have never been happier by myself. Aiden rarely calls, and a lot of the time, when he does, I cut the conversation short, saying I need to change a diaper or feed Josalyn, or on a couple of occasions, I've ignored the call. We have absolutely nothing to talk about. He obligingly asks about the baby, but I can tell he's always anxious to hurry the conversation up so he can get back to playing his games. Brittany told me they're able to get bootleg games over there for super cheap, so I have no doubt he's having a blast during his off time.

I'm not just content right now; I'm actually happy. There's nothing better than spending the day with my baby girl. My mom, granny, and I spend all hours of the day doting on her. I have no doubt she's going to be spoiled rotten, but we just can't help it. She is the sweetest little thing, the perfect baby. And she's all mine.

Kayla's Chick Rant & Book Blog
July 5, 2007

My mom, Anni, and I took Josalyn to see the fireworks at Ft. Bragg last night. She jumped after the first one cracked in the sky, but when she caught sight of the bright explosions lighting up the sky, she was mesmerized. I spent so much time watching her reactions and adorable facial expressions that I barely saw any of the fireworks myself.

    Afterward, I put Josalyn to bed at nine, brought my mom the baby monitor, and went out for the first time in forever. Anni and I met my cousins at It'z, where we sat on the patio and listened to live music. I only had a glass of red wine since I'm breastfeeding, but being out with my best friend again felt amazing. It was the first time I felt comfortable leaving Josalyn. The only time I've left her has been just long enough to run to the top of the hill in Hope Mills to grab some fast food and bring it back home.

    Just like I thought, I finished my class assignments way early, and was actually able to sign up for a summer-mini. I was worried about taking a class crammed into four weeks, so I only have one, sociology.

I still haven't heard anything from Jason since before his birthday in January. I kept thinking he might at least message me congratulating me on Josalyn, but he never did. On his profile, I see he's dating some chick who is obsessed with astrology. She posts all sorts of star sign crap on his page, and they call each other things like, "my fire" and "my air," referring to her being an Aries and him being an Aquarius. I've always been one who loves gooey romance, but it makes even me vomity. But I'm sure if it were anyone else besides Jason, it wouldn't make me sick.

I have absolutely no hope of us ever being together, but for the first time in two years, it's not a crushing, debilitating pain. Don't get me wrong; it still hurts, like I'm missing a part of myself, but I now have the ability to force it out of my head when the ache starts to grow too strong. I miss having him to talk to. I'd be happy with our old friendship, just messaging back and forth, but I can't expect him to take the time to email me when he's obviously in a happy relationship with some other girl.

I have someone more important to worry about now, instead of just myself. My focus is all on Josalyn, making sure she will have anything she could possibly ever want. That's why I'm going to work my ass off and make something of myself. My goal is to not need anyone—not my parents, not Aiden, not a single person but me. I'm going to finish up my degree and write, fulfill the dreams I had before I ever got caught up with stupid boys.

Mark my words, peeps. I'll be an author one day. God only knows how long it'll take me, but I know it'll happen. Someday.

CHAPTER Twenty-One

I say that I don't care and walk away, whatever

August 29, 2007

    Instead of waiting on Aiden to get back from deployment, I'm going ahead with finding a house to rent and moving into it. There's no need to wait. It's not like he ever helps the moving process anyway, and this way I won't have to deal with his input.

    I find the cutest three-bedroom house very close to my parents', only about five minutes away. The rent is within our budget, and with my power of attorney, I'm able to get all the rental agreements signed and completed. It's only a six-month lease, which is perfect since we don't know if or when Aiden will be picked to either deploy or get based somewhere else.

I dread the day we get the news we have to move somewhere else. In fact, I've seriously thought of telling him I'd just stay here in Fayetteville when he gets his new station. He'll just get deployed anyway, and I'd be stuck in another state by myself. Fuck that. Actually, in all honesty, I wouldn't mind being a single mom one bit. But that's being selfish. Josalyn shouldn't have to grow up in a broken home.

I don't really know what it'll be like when he gets home, since we have such a set routine. I won't tolerate him coming in and just trying to take over, changing everything we've perfected with our routine. I'd rather it be a roommate situation. You go about your business, and I'll go about mine. We'll work as a team when we need it, but other than that, don't fucking mess with me. I'll be over here doing my schoolwork, and you go play your adolescent little game, and we'll all be happy.

I especially love the house, because it's three bedrooms. For the short time we lived at my parents' together right before Josalyn was born and then before he deployed again, it was awkward sleeping in the same bed with him. When he was home before, he always slept on the couch, because he'd stay up all hours playing. And then while he was in the desert, I slept by myself, of course. With the third bedroom, I can make it a clear point that we wouldn't be sharing a bed at any point anymore.

It would be nice having our own separate space too. He could keep all his crap in his room, and then I could decorate mine however I wanted, without worrying if he thinks the bedding is too feminine or he has enough room in the closet.

My brother Jay and my dad are going to help me move in a little less than two weeks, right before Aiden gets home. I'll be able to get everything set up how I want it, without having to argue with him. I don't know why he always tries to dictate where things go. I swear I think he just likes to feel like he has some kind of power over me. He doesn't truly care that the bed is on the wall with the window, or the bookcase is on the opposite side from the TV. I think he just likes to argue, getting some type of enjoyment out of upsetting me. Last time we moved, I flat out told him that since he didn't help me pack everything up, he had no right to tell me where everything went when we unpacked at my parents'. I wasn't going to deal with his shit. But this time, I wouldn't even have to have that annoying conversation, because I'd have it all done before he got home.

I'm taking more classes at one time than I have since my semester in Texas. I've been able to keep on top of everything, holding all four of my courses at a steady A. I'm trying to bust out as many hard ones as I can now, that way my last couple of semesters will be easy. Also, I'm trying to do as many online courses as possible too.

My mom said she'd be more than willing to keep Josalyn while I'm at school, but I just can't bring myself to leave her yet. She'll be four months old tomorrow, and I'm still breastfeeding her. I'm scared if I spend hours away from her, it'll fuck up the routine we have down, and also mess with my milk production. Not to mention, it fucking hurts when I go too long without feeding her. I don't know why, but my boobs just don't like pumps. I can only get about four ounces out, and that's barely enough for one feeding. I've made it this long without using formula, so I don't want to start now.

I have absolutely nothing against people who use formula; shit, I wasn't breastfed, but the benefits of breast milk are all the incentive I need to let my daughter keep using me as her own personal vending machine. I'll get my body back to myself when she's a year. I'll stop then, when there's really no beneficial reason to keep doing it besides the closeness you get with your little one.

Maybe after this semester, I'll give it a go and sign up for classes on campus, but for now, I'm going to enjoy crawling into bed in my pajamas with my laptop and doing my assignments while Josalyn snoozes beside me in her crib.

Kayla's Chick Rant & Book Blog
September 12, 2007

Been so busy the past two weeks I haven't had much time to

update y'all. For the first time in three years, my birthday was *awesome!* I mean, it wasn't anything spectacular, but it was so much fun. I put Josalyn to bed at 9 p.m. as usual, kissed Mom and Granny goodbye, and then Anni, Brittany, and I went to this new Irish pub that opened up in town called Paddy's. The owner, whose name really is Paddy, is from Ireland, and he and his musical partner Bill play live music every night. Paddy plays the guitar, Bill plays the electric violin, and they both sing everything you can imagine.

They played show-stopping renditions of "The Devil Went Down to Georgia" and "Sweet Child of Mine," but the best was when they played "Take On Me" and pulled me up on stage to play the tambourine when Anni yelled it was my birthday. I've always loved that song. My dad has it on a 45 record and would play it every Sunday afternoon when we'd get home from church. We'd dance in the living room while Granny complained the music was too loud.

I was a rebel and drank *two* glasses of wine, but after being pregnant for nine months, and then breastfeeding for four and a half, I'm a lightweight and was totally sloshed. Anni grabbed me off the stage just in time before I followed Paddy's Irish drinking song's instructions when everyone yelled, "Show us your tits!"

We laughed all night long at the songs about foreskins and Irishmen drinking too much, sang along to "Zombie" by The Cranberries, and about bust a gut every time a girl would pass by the stage to get to the restroom, and Paddy would screech the song to a halt to tell her, "No number twos in there, sweetheart," or "Schwing...schwingidy, schwing-

schwing," if she was particularly good-looking. It was the best night I'd had in a very long time.

Surprisingly, after Anni got me home safe and sound, waking up with Josalyn wasn't as painful as I thought it was going to be. Thank goodness for that "Mommy chip" in my brain I read about. A mother's instinct is a mysterious and miraculous thing. I move into the new house tomorrow, and then Aiden gets home two days later. Anni is going to come over and help me unpack after my dad and brother get all the furniture and boxes moved in. I'll post pictures of my new set up! I found some new bookcases to put in *my* room. No more keeping them in cardboard boxes because the douche canoe says they take up too much space. Blasphemy!

CHAPTER Twenty-Two

Just gotta get past the midnight hour

September 14, 2007

Five-hundred sixty-five dollars and ninety-six cents. My heart leapt into my chest when I found the Wal-Mart receipt in the bathroom's little trashcan. I had ran in here about to wet myself after spending the last couple of hours washing, drying, folding, and putting away clothes, and when I happened to glance over to replace the toilet paper roll, there it was. A receipt for $565.96 spent on a brand new PlayStation 3.

My hands begin to shake as the argument we had the very day he got home from deployment flashed through my mind. We'd had a screaming match over a diaper bag I'd wanted. Yes, it was pretty extravagant, nearly two hundred bucks for a diaper bag, but hell, I deserved it! I'd been working my ass off at school, plus I was considering it a birthday present from Aiden, since he hadn't bothered sending me anything while he was still overseas.

He was so pissed off at me, screaming at me and waking Josalyn up, that I finally gave in and told him I'd return it. I was so angry I cried. They were furious tears, and I hated to let him see he got to me like that.

I pull my phone out of my pocket and look at the time. 8:27 p.m. Aiden had switched shifts and was now working from 7 p.m. to 7 a.m. I had just laid Josalyn down in her crib, but as the immediate idea hit me, I didn't give two shits if I woke her up. I storm into the living room and grab her carrier then bring it into her nursery. I gently pick her up, kissing her plump little cheek before getting her all strapped into her car seat.

"We're going for a little ride, baby girl," I whisper to her, not wanting her to fully awaken, but needing to speak to someone, anyone, before I burst with the adrenaline pumping through me.

I set her carrier into its base in my back seat, making sure it locks into place, and then crank up my Malibu, feeling a spike of glee slice through me. I hook my headphone over my ear and call Anni. When she answers, I immediately start ranting.

"That mother*fucker!* He has the audacity to force me to return my birthday present, and then the shithead has the balls to go out and spend almost six hundred bucks on a fucking game console?! I'll be fucking damned! I swear to God, he's going to make me end up on an episode of *America's Most Wanted*! I'm going to fucking snap, Anni."

"Where are you? You sound like you're driving. Where's Josalyn?" she rushes out.

"As soon as I found the receipt, I got her out of her crib and put her in the car. Our happy asses are going to the bank," I tell her. I can actually feel the wildness in my eyes.

"You're upset, girl. You need to calm down with that baby in your car. Think of your little one," Anni says soothingly.

I'm stopped at a stoplight, so I take in her words and take a deep breath, letting it all sink in. She's right. They say driving upset is just as bad as driving drunk. I need to chill the hell out, so I don't put my girl in danger. After a few more calming breaths, the light turns green, and I take off at a normal speed, when before I would've probably burned rubber.

"I'm good. I'm going to the ATM and taking out my fair share, goddammit. I can only take out $500 at a time, but you bet your sweet ass I'll be getting the difference tomorrow. That motherfucker has messed with me for the last time," I vow.

"Well, stay on the phone with me until you get home. I don't like you going to an ATM by yourself when it's dark."

"Yes, mother," I tease.

I pull into the bank's parking lot and around to the drive-up ATM. I put in my pin number after swiping my card, and a thrill shoots through me as I push the button on the screen for $500. When it shoots out my twenties, I squeal excitedly and put it in my purse in the passenger seat. Tomorrow, I'll go open up my own damn account. Something tells me I need to start saving up as much money as I possibly can.

Not an hour later, Aiden calls me in hysterics, having checked the bank account like some obsessed stalker. I can't wipe the smile off my face as I tell him evilly, "We're married, Aiden. Everything is fifty-fifty. So unless you want me to use your brand new PlayStation 3 you hid in your room as target practice with Granny's shotgun, you're gonna shut your fucking mouth and drop it."

Having been around my hormonal wrath while I was pregnant, when I had a tendency to throw and break things, preferably near his giant head, he knew I wasn't messing around. He didn't bring it up again.

The next day, I don't bother going to the ATM to withdraw the rest of the money. I go back to the boutique and rebuy my adorable diaper bag.

September 25, 2007

Ten days.

Ten fucking days we've been officially moved into this house, and I'm already done. I have absolutely had it. There is no coming back from this. Not that I thought Aiden and I would ever be a happily married couple. But this? I can't be married to a person who I look at and absolutely hate.

Hate is a strong word, and some would say it's wrong to say you hate someone. But at this very moment, I hate Aiden with every fiber of my being. You can neglect and ignore me, whatever. I'm a big girl; I don't fucking need you. But you do it to my baby girl, I'll fucking kill you before you ever get a chance to do it again.

I took the day off from school because I had a lot of errands to run today, so I asked Aiden if he'd watch Josalyn while I went and got everything done before he went to work at two. It was around 9:30 a.m., and I put her in her high chair after I finished nursing her, placing a couple of her favorite toys on the tray in front of her.

"I pumped enough for you to feed her if she starts getting fussy before I get back. It's in the fridge," I told him as I rolled her high chair next to the couch, where Aiden sat with his headphones on, playing one of his shooter games. He didn't answer me, so I stepped in front of the TV, finally getting his attention.

"What?" he asked, trying to look around my body.

"Are you going to be able to handle this? Or should I just take her with me?" I inquired.

"Nah, she's good. Go get your shit done."

"Did you hear what I said about her bottle?"

"In the fridge," he mumbled, and I rolled my eyes and stepped away from the TV. I walked back over to Josalyn and gave her a bunch of kisses all over her face, and after receiving the giggle I wanted, I grabbed my purse and headed out the door.

I had a ton of things to get done, quick things, but a lot of different places, so it would've been a hassle parking, unloading the stroller from the trunk, getting Josalyn's carrier out of its base, doing whatever stop I was at, and then reloading everything back into the car. Then, throwing in diaper changes and a feeding to slow me down, all I wanted was to get all my crap done fast so I could enjoy the rest of my day home with my girl.

I went to my school and turned in a project I had to do for one of my online classes. I went to the DMV and finally renewed my driver's license, which expired on my birthday a couple weeks ago. I returned a couple baby outfits Josalyn never wore that still had the tags on them, trading them for the size she'd be in next. I got my oil changed at my cousin's car dealership, and finally ran through Wal-Mart for some groceries.

When I walked in the door, arms loaded down with plastic bags of food, it was the smell that hit me first. Had Riley had an upset stomach? I looked around the floor for doggy diarrhea, but there was none in sight. Then it was the silence inside the house that caused my heart to skip a beat. Aiden's game was on the start menu on the TV, but he was nowhere in sight. His car was outside, so I knew he was home, and as I listened more closely, I heard the water running in the very back of the house.

I dropped the bags on the kitchen floor and headed to the bedroom to see if he might be giving the baby a bath or something. Maybe the smell was an exploded diaper and he was cleaning her up.

Instead, what I found scared me more than I've ever felt in my life. It was Aiden in the shower, but that wasn't what terrified me. Josalyn wasn't there. She wasn't in the bouncy chair sitting on the bathroom floor, where I keep her when I take a shower.

I slammed the bathroom door against the wall in my panic to find her, making Aiden shout and throw back the shower curtain. "You scared the shit out of me," he said with a short burst of laughter. His face fell when he saw the look on mine, and he asked, "What's wrong?"

"Where is my baby?" I questioned in a voice that would spark fear in the manliest of men.

"What do you mean where is she? She's in the high chair. You had to walk right past her when you came in," he replied, giving me a stupid look.

I didn't even listen to whatever else he had to say. I ran as fast as my legs could move, and when I got back into the living room, there was my poor, sweet little five-month-old baby girl, slumped over asleep in the high chair, where I had sat her nearly four hours ago.

Tears filled my eyes as I ran to her. I held my breath as I removed the tray with one hand, holding her upright with the other. I sat it on the couch next to us and then unbuckled the belt around her tiny little waist. Reaching under her arms, I lifted her from the chair and pulled her to my body, and her stretch and sigh against my chest allowed me to take my first full breath since I saw her.

There was wetness at her back, and when I looked down, I saw her onesie was soaked through with poop. I hurried to her bathroom, not bothering to take her to the changing table in her nursery because there was such a mess, and I sat on the toilet, laying her across my legs. By now, she was waking up, and when I looked at her face and beside her beautiful hazel eyes, I could see she had been crying, probably wearing herself out until she fell asleep like that. I wiped at the crusted tears that had dried in the outer corners, and more tears of my own formed.

When she first looked up and saw me, her face lit up like it always did, and I felt both relieved and guilty. I should have known better than to leave her with that asshole. I should have just taken her with me. Yes, it would have taken longer to get my stuff done, but at least she would have been safe.

"Let's get you cleaned up, pretty girl," I whispered to her, a teardrop falling and landing on her onesie as I unsnapped the buttons between her legs. I carefully rolled the fabric as I pulled it up, trapping the excrement inside so it wouldn't smear as I pulled it over her head. It was so full I didn't even want to bother washing it, so I just pushed it into the top of the Diaper Genie. Next, I took her diaper off, rolling it with one hand and then putting it into the Diaper Genie as well. I didn't care I was getting the poop all over my legs, especially when I saw how red she was all over her privates and butt. And in that moment, that wasn't the only red I was seeing. That was the very second every ounce of me filled with hate for the man who was supposed to be taking care of my baby while I was running errands.

    I stood and placed Josalyn in her bath seat in the tub while I frantically took my clothes off as fast as I could. I turned on the water and got it to the perfect temperature, picked her back up, and held her steadily under the running water, washing away all the mess. After removing her bath seat, I carefully stepped into the tub and rinsed off my legs where she had laid across them, and when it was all off, I used the shower head to clean out the tub before pushing in the stopper and filling it with her lavender-scented soapy water.

    I don't know how long I laid there in the tub with her against my chest, using her pink cup to pour water over her precious little butt, where I could see the terrible burn rash that had formed from sitting in her dirty diaper for so long. It wasn't until I heard Aiden come in from the garage, where he always threw his uniform into the dryer before work that I pulled myself together and got out. I placed her in her bath seat while I wrapped a towel around myself, and then grabbed her up in one of her hooded towels, swaddling her up tight so she wouldn't get chilled.

I took her into her room and got her dressed, making sure to slather her in lots of diaper rash ointment. The angry red still showing through the thick white salve. I sat in the rocking chair next to her crib, and I rocked and nursed her until she fell into a nice, deep sleep. I didn't want to let her go, but I also didn't want her to be around what was about to happen, so I laid her down in her crib and smiled when she let out a big sigh as she stretched out. I glanced at the baby monitor on her dresser to make sure the light was on, and then left the room, pulling her door closed behind me.

The simple fact Aiden hadn't bothered to come check on us the entire time I've been home fixing what he'd done only adds to the fire inside me. Rage like I've never felt consumes me as I stalk into the bedroom, where he is sitting in the chair by the window putting on his work boots.

"You motherfucker," I growl, feeling my entire body trembling with emotion.

He looks up at me in question, but I don't give him time to speak before I blow up.

"I have had it with you. I am done! I was willing to live unhappily in order for Josalyn to grow up with both parents, but after what you did today, it would be better for her to have a broken home than a father who would let that happen to her. It's your job to keep her safe, to take care of her and keep her from getting hurt. You did none of that today. None of it! I couldn't even run some errands for a few hours without you melting the skin off my baby!" I scream the last few words, and his eyes grow wide.

"What are you talking about?" he asks, and it only

stokes the inferno inside me.

"Not only did you leave our five-month-old in a goddamn high chair for almost four hours, but you let her sit in her shit for that long, and it burned all her skin. She basically sat in acid for God only knows how long, while you were nowhere in sight! Why the fuck didn't you get her out of there when she was crying. And don't tell me she wasn't crying, because I could see the dried tears on her face!"

"Yeah, she was crying, so I did what you said and gave her the bottle. I had to get ready for work, so while she was quiet, I hopped in the shower," he says defensively.

"So let me get this straight. You left her by herself in the high chair on the opposite side of the house, drinking her bottle, while you got into the shower, where you wouldn't be able to see or hear it if she got choked? *Even better!* Do you have no fucking common sense? She's five months old! I never leave her in her high chair longer than about twenty minutes. She barely just learned to hold herself up, and you left her there for four goddamn hours!" I rage.

"She was strapped in. It's not like she could fall out," he tells me.

"Let me guess. You played your fucking video games the whole time I was gone, while she just sat there. You couldn't put down the fucking game long enough to play with her a little? To let her out and at least play on the floor in front of you? You didn't think to check her diaper in *four fucking hours*? You can't tell me you didn't smell it!"

"It was just about time for you to get home, and I needed to get ready for work, so I figured you could just change her when you came in," he confesses, having the decency to look a little sheepish.

"Please, tell me just how long 'just about time for me to get home' means? Because she had to have been like that for a while for it to burn her that badly," I challenge.

He rubs the back of his neck and tries to flub his answer. "Oh, I don't know for sure. I was playing my game, and you know my time gets all messed up when I play. It couldn't have been more than like, thirty minutes."

"One, there's no way that amount of damage to her skin could have happened in just thirty minutes. And two, even if it was only half an hour, what kind of father lets their baby sit in their shit for that long?" I shake my head and look him dead in the eye. "I'm done. I'm not doing this anymore."

"What do you mean? What are you saying?" he asks quietly.

"I'm saying I want a divorce."

Kayla's Chick Rant & Book Blog
October 1, 2007

First, I want to thank everyone for their comments of support after I vented the other day about what my soon-to-be ex-husband did to my daughter. Before I read the comments, I worried people would think I was overreacting to a dirty diaper, but y'all made me feel so much better, and like my mommy instincts were right.

I'd like to mention some of these comments, in case some of you didn't catch them before the thread got so long.

Rosie: "Oh, you've got me a blubbering mess. He is awful. I hate him!"
Thank you, Rosie. If I wasn't so royally pissed off, I would have been blubbering harder for my baby girl as well.

Carrie: "You should've punched him hard in the junk after delivering the divorce line...what a complete asshole. Wow!"
Lord, did I want to! It's like one of those things where you think of a really good comeback way after a fight. Totally should have accented that blow with a kick to the balls!

Kali: OMG! Hate is a very strong word. I always tell my kids, "You don't hate anybody; you can strongly dislike them, but you don't hate them." Screw that. If anyone deserves a 'hate,' it's him. How can you do that? Poor little baby.
Kali, I thought I'd felt that emotion before, but after that

happened, I now know what true hate feels like. You sound like a great mommy!

Stacia: OMG, what a douche! I can't even...poor Josalyn! I'm with Carrie. Please tell us you did junk punch him at some point...?

The most violent thing my little body has ever done is throw a remote control as hard as I could at his big-ass head. Unfortunately, my non-athleticism showed and I missed. We'll see how the divorce goes though. I'll keep you updated. *wink*

Rhonda: You had every right to get that mad over what he did! Anyone who doesn't think it's justified obviously don't have kids and have never dealt with any kind of severe diaper rash. I felt awful when my boys would have a tummy bug and their diapers would be just liquid! They would get all red and raw, and that would be from sitting in it for just minutes—until they fussed, I heard it, or smelled it. To know she sat in a dirty diaper for over an hour would be so painful for her little body. Side note: I need to know if this motherfucker ever got junk punched, bitch slapped, or at least an atomic wedgie. Have you told Anni? I'm sure she'd have no problem doing it!

Rhonda, thank you so much for your comment. You have no idea how much better your experience with your kids makes me feel. It was absolutely heartbreaking seeing her skin like that. And she's such a sweet-natured baby; it broke my heart even more that this would happen to her. Atomic wedgie? OMG, I just died! No, I haven't told Anni. I don't want my bestie to end up in jail.

Melody: What an asshole! Actually, that is a nice name for him! How could anyone be so selfish to leave their 5-month-old baby strapped in a high chair? And to leave her sitting in her waste on top of that, because he's too lazy and too obsessed with video games? UGH! Kayla, I'm surprised you didn't punch him the hell out.

I'm starting to notice a running theme here. My blog followers are a bunch of violent mama bears, and I freaking LOVE it! Note to self: when all else fails, punch a motherfucker!

Morgan: I'm so glad I kicked my sperm donor to the curb while I was still pregnant. I just know that would have been something he did. Poor baby girl.

Morgan, good for you! I wish I would've had the sense sooner. That's what I get for being an idiot and marrying a guy after only knowing him a few months.

*Kolleen: Poor sweet baby Josalyn *sad face*.*

Jennifer: I only have dogs, but I'd still kick a motherfucker's ass.

Thank you, Kolleen and Jennifer! And it's especially nice to hear from a mom of only furbabies that I didn't overreact.

Vanessa: I would have kicked his ass. MUTHAFUKA leaving that poor baby like that... It made me so mad when I read what happened to your princess in your post. I'm glad you're divorcing that prick. Sorry for being so NY Puerto Rican ghetto. But I hate when shit like that happens to innocent children who have no way of speaking up. Kids always come first.

Vanessa, first, no apologies needed. If I'm ever in a

fight, I'm calling you! Second, I have a blog follower all the way up in NY? How cool is that?! Thank you for your comment.

So, I decided since we just moved into this house and it has a six-month lease, we're both going to stay, but only because we have separate rooms. I rarely see him anyway, thanks to his work schedule, and then he hides out playing his video games and poker tournaments when he's off. I just know better than to leave Josalyn alone with him now. It'll be a roommate situation, but this time without the benefits, if you could even call them that in the first place. *snort*

Enough about that. Want to hear a funny story?
The other day, Mom and I wanted to go see a movie at the dollar theatre, so we left Josalyn with Granny. We had about thirty minutes to kill, so we decided to peruse the sex shop across the street from the theatre. Some of you might think that's weird, to go to the sex shop with your mom, but if you knew her, you'd know I get my craziness from her. I snuck off with her romance novels when I was little, remember?

Anyway, we get in there, and are walking around the perimeter, where all the stripper outfits are, and then we get to the men's section. There were these black, pin-stripe, spandex booty shorts that felt really slick, and running her hand over it, my mom said, "Ohhhh, I bet these would feel good on a man's ass!" Being who I am, my immediate response was to glance around the store, and that's when I spotted what I was looking for—a group of unsuspecting soldiers in the porn section.

I grabbed the undies off the hook and started making my way over to them, my mom whisper-hissing, "KD, don't you dare!" as I skipped ahead. I walked up to the five relatively good-looking guys and asked their group, "Hey, boys. My mom over there"—I pointed at her and waved, at which point she turned red all the way up through her blonde scalp—"would like to know what this would feel like on a man's ass. Any one of you willing to try them on for her?"

They all looked at each other, smiling and chuckling, until one snatched it out of my hand, saying, "Shit, why not?" His buddies laughed harder and patted him on the back, and then he made his way to the dressing room. I followed him over, while my mom tried her best to hide behind the boas and nipple pasties.

After a few minutes, I heard the soldier call out, "Okay! I have them on. They're a little...tight!"

"Even better!" I yelled to him, and he opened the curtain.

My head tilted at the sight of his ripped, tattooed body, his junk barely contained within the tiny piece of stretchy fabric. "Very nice," is all I managed to get out before I hollered across the store, "Mom, get your ass over here! He put them on for you!"

Bright red and giggling like a schoolgirl, my adorably embarrassed mom scurried over to where I stood with the brave man.

"Okay, will you model them for her?" I prompted.

The dude turned around and literally shook his booty in my mom's direction, making us and all of his friends, who had now gathered around for the show, laugh hysterically. Then, the most epic thing happened.

My sweet, tiny, blonde, innocent looking, sixty-year-old mother asked him, "Can I feel them?"

My jaw almost hit the floor, and at the same time, the soldier nodded, jutted his hip out, sticking out a cheek for her to rub. I watched in pure astonished pride as my mom groped the very well-developed hiney of the shameless soldier.

God Bless Our Troops.

Chapter Twenty-Three

October 20, 2007

I'm just going to start calling Jenna my personal employment service. Wanting to distance myself as much as I possibly can, and also wanting to be able to stand on my own two feet, I decided I need to get a job. Yes, I'd be super busy trying to keep up with both work and school while raising a baby by myself, but at least I knew I had my mom and granny when I truly needed them.

Jenna had quit her job at GNC a long time ago, and was now the office manager of a family-owned heating and air conditioning company. When she saw I had asked on MySpace if any of my friends knew of any office jobs available, she immediately messaged me saying she was looking for an appointment dispatcher. The only setback I could see was that it's a full-time job. I'd work from seven to five every day, which was a lot more than I planned on working when I have a baby to raise and school.

I talked to my mom about it, and she said she was more than willing to watch Josalyn while I was at work. Jenna is the one who hired me, so the only 'interview' I had was just a meeting with the owner's son to fill out all the employment paperwork. There was a lot of downtime with this job, so I'd be able to do schoolwork while I was there.

I feel like a brand new person, waking up early, taking my daughter to my mom's house, stopping for coffee on my way to my full-time job, in which I get to sit across a desk from my good friend all day. While she handles all the billing and accounts, I set and keep track of all heating and a/c appointments. I communicate with our technicians on a walkie-talkie, giving them the address to their next repair or maintenance appointment. So between dispatching, I have about an hour to get school assignments done before I have to call them with their next address.

It's also the most money I've ever made in my life. I make ten dollars an hour! And all of it is getting socked away in my new personal bank account. As soon as my divorce is final, I know I won't have any problem making it on my own. Who needs a fucking man?

Kayla's Chick Rant & Book Blog
November 13, 2007

That fucking motherfucker. That fucking shitheaded fuckstick. I can't even come up with a name hateful enough to describe the asshole also known as my soon-to-be ex-husband.

HE. ORDERED. A. PATERNITY. TEST.

Yeah. You read that correctly. That fucking dicklicker had the audacity to send me a court-ordered paternity test for our daughter, who, mind you, came out of me looking EXACTLY like his dumb ass. My poor girl. Please, dear Lord, let her grow out of that. That baby looks like you sawed off his stupid face and sewed it on her, *Face/Off* style, and he has the gall to send me a paternity test?

He tried to claim his lawyer told him he had to, but it's funny how it all came about when we were discussing child support. Everything else is completely amicable. No fighting over anything. I'll take Josalyn and our shit, and he can keep the rest. I don't want anything else from him. But when I showed him the amount the online calculator came up with for the child support he'd owe me monthly, he went quiet. A few days later, I get a letter stating I have to have a paternity test before child support will be confirmed.

So yesterday, I took my sweet, precious little baby girl up to the lab, meeting Aiden there, since I got off from work early for the appointment. When the technician took one look at Josalyn, and then over at Aiden, he scoffed, saying, "Why would you spend hundreds of dollars on this test when you can just glance at that baby and see she's definitely yours?" He was an older gentleman, and I couldn't help but laugh at his bluntness.

"You win the award for my favorite person of the day," I told the man cheerfully, and then glared over at Aiden, who looked embarrassed. Good. I hoped he felt like the complete ass he was being. Just the implication that Josalyn could be someone else's, not just because she looks so much like Aiden, but the simple fact that while he and I were trying to get pregnant, he had me locked up in our apartment like fucking Rapunzel, pissed me the hell off. I'm glad I had someone else, especially a total stranger, on my side.

In the end, he swabbed her cheek, and then Aiden's, and told us the results would be in in a couple of weeks. I left with Josalyn without saying anything to Aiden, while he sat writing a hefty check to the lab. If he wanted to spend all that money on a pointless test as opposed to his stupid video games, he could go right ahead. It wouldn't affect me anymore in the slightest.

About the Author

KD Robichaux wanted to be a romance author since the first time she picked up her mom's Sandra Brown books at the ripe old age of twelve. She went to college to become a writer, but then married and had babies. Putting her dream job on hold to raise her family as a stay at home mom, who read entirely too much, she created a blog where she could keep her family and friends up-to-date on all the hottest reads. From there, by word of mouth, her blog took off and she began using her hard-earned degree as a Senior Editor for Hot Tree Editing. When her kids started school, and with the encouragement from her many author friends, she finally sat down and started working on her first series, The Blogger Diaries, her very own real life romance.

If you're interested in getting your hands on upcoming releases, sneak peek teasers, or information on my upcoming personal appearances, and sales, you can join me on the social media links below.

Facebook:
https://www.facebook.com/AuthorKDRobichaux
Twitter:
@kaylaTheBiblio
Instagram:
Kaylathebibliophile

ACKN♠WLEDGEMENTS

Book Two was so much harder to write than the first one. After publishing *Wished for You*, finally completing it after spending almost two years writing it, the sense of relief completion brought was instantly taken away by the pending doom that was *Wish He Was You*. I had the thought, *Oh shit. I just finished. You mean I have to start all over again?*

Looking back, now that *WHWY* is all finished, I believe it was the content that made me feel overwhelmed. It was not a very happy time in my life. And now, looking forward to book three, *Wish Come True*, I feel a sense of excitement I didn't feel at the beginning of *WHWY*. I cannot wait to not only complete my trilogy, but to finally tell the world my happily ever after. Even if it isn't the perfect tale of rainbows and butterflies, it's real, and I wouldn't have had it any other way, because it makes me appreciate what I have now with my wonderful husband and beautiful daughters (yes, daughters is plural. SPOILER ALERT, hehe!)

Four months after publishing *Wished for You*, I finally gained the courage to put fingers back to the keys (Fall Out Boy reference intended), and man, was it coming easily! I was busting out around 6k words a day, and for those of you who do not write, that's a pretty good chunk of writing for one day.

But then, on day four into my journey of book 2, I got the worst news of my entire life. My sweet, amazing, wonderful Granny, who you got to meet in this story, passed away peacefully in her sleep. One of the things that's always made me feel guilty about moving to Texas to start my life was leaving behind my family and friends in NC, most of all my granny and Mom. Since I grew up with Granny living with us, we always had a much closer bond than most people do with their grandparents, made even stronger by the fact she was the only grandparent I ever had. And with this news came two months of the most impenetrable writer's block. It's like the words just left me; my hands stopped typing. I couldn't edit or even read for pleasure.

But then, a little light. It was time for the RT Convention, and I got to spend nearly a week being roommates with one of my best friends, my Twinnie, Erin Noelle. One night, instead of staying up all hours drooling over authors like Sandra Brown and EL James from across the bar, we were good girls, went to bed early, and I wrote my little heart out for the first time in months. Just having her there to encourage me to get back to it was enough to kick my ass back in gear. At the end of our writing spree, I looked over at her and said with pride and astonishment, "I just wrote 3k," to which she replied, "I wrote a paragraph...but DAMN it's a great ass paragraph!" Lol!

When I got back home from Dallas, I asked my friend Stephanie Garza if she'd like to sprint, because I noticed she always seemed so enthusiastic to write, and I wanted a little bit of her positivity to rub off on me. Sure enough, sending selfies to each other in front of our computers and messaging, "You ready? 3...2...1...GO!" was really all it took to make writing fun again. I learned if you really pay attention, and weed through all the negativity some people post on FB, you'll begin to notice those few you can call your tribe, the ones who are there to lift their friends up, even if it's unintentional; it's just who they are.

My Beta Girls. Dear Lord, where would I be without y'all? We blew up messenger so bad we had to make a Secret Group just so we could keep up with each other! FUN FACT! The "blog follower comments" I answer during the blog post about the dirty diaper were actually the comments made by my beautiful beta girls in our private group after they read that scene in my book.

Speaking of my beta girls:

Kolleen Oxbury, thank you for being Canadian. The Canada scene was hard enough to write, so I'm so thankful I had you to keep my details on point!

"I'm glad everyone's balls are now where they are supposed to be." —Kali McQuillen (I love you, woman!)

Stacia Mitchell, you have an eye for detail that makes my little editor heart proud.

Jennifer Severino, thank you for keeping me out of jail. It's pretty awesome to have a lawyer as a friend and beta, and I love that you are just little bit evil like me <3

Melody Dawn, thank you for always being the first person to volunteer to help me with anything. You are truly the most selfless person I know.

The rest of my beta girls—Carrie, Kylie, Morgan,

Rhonda, Theresa, JD, and Vanessa, —thank you so much for keeping me going! Every time I'd send you the next few chapters, y'all always begged for more. There isn't a better feeling than that.

There are a special few women who come to mind when I think of who I want to acknowledge, and they are the ones who when I open my notifications on my author page, there are HUNDREDS of comments of where they have pimped me out. There are an infinite number of authors in the world, and yet they choose to spread the word about little ole me. Rosie Snowdon, Franci Neill, and Kali (again, you're kinda the shit), seriously, no one would know who the heck I am if it weren't for y'all. Thank you for pimping your little hearts out. I appreciate you so much.

Heather Lane, not only do you make the greatest book trailers in all the land, (shout out to Book Obsession Production), but you have a way of keeping me on my game. "FaceTime with me for an hour...but then get your ass to work on that book!" hehe! Thank you for helping me keep up with my real blog, Kayla the Bibliophile, and for everything else you do. I'll keep feeding you Chuy's and keep you stocked with signed paperbacks.

Tina Hernandez, your excitement always gets me pumped to write more. You're so animated with your passion for books, and I'm so glad we are a part of the same team. There's no one I'd recommend more, and I'm happy to share my Hot Tree tribe with you. Who knew years and years ago, when we met in our college elective Yoga class, that we'd end up here? Love you, girl!

Becky Johnson, you are the boss above all other bosses. I am seriously blessed to have you not only as my head honcho, but as my friend and cheerleader. You may literally be on the other side of the planet, but I feel closer to you than some friends just right down the street. When this book is released on Avary's birthday, August 21, it will be less than two months until I get to meet you in person for the very first time. Prepare for the tackle-hug of your life, "lovely xx" <3

My Jamie-Boo, you are the best best friend a girl could ever ask for. You keep me centered and always keep me laughing. If days go by and you don't hear from me, you make sure I'm still alive deep in my writing cave, send me a few chuckles, and then leave me to it, knowing my ass will come back around eventually. Ours is an effortless friendship, and I love you so much, my sister from another mister.

Speaking of sisters…when I was trying to figure out what name to give my ex, I asked Jamie, "When you were younger, who was the biggest asshole to you?" expecting her to give me the name of a childhood bully or something. Negative. She answered, "My big sister Amber." So that is how we came up with Aiden's last name, giving him Amber's, Lanmon. Amber, thanks for being a big jerk back in the day, and thank you for being pretty damn awesome nowadays. Nothing makes me laugh harder than reading y'all's banter on Facebook.

Sara Ferguson, words can't describe how much I adore you. It's probably a good thing we don't live in the same state. The world wouldn't be able to handle alla-dat.

Kristen Bauer, Jason's very first fangirl. Thank you for giving me the idea of "I'm a Ho for Robichaux" as swag!

Barbara "Blue Kitty" Johnson, my feelings would probably still be in shambles if you hadn't turned my broken heart over a bad review into the best inside joke in the world. My favorite #whore of them all.

Shawna "ZombieQueen" Stringer, my oldest book world friend, I'm so glad that when you FINALLY read *Wished for You*, I had just finished *Wish He Was You*, because I probably would have had to fear for my life for leaving you on the original cliffhanger. There's no one I'd rather have by my side during the apocalypse.

Surprisingly, I have to give credit to Erin's husband Zar yet again, but this time it isn't because he's playing the "other man" on my book cover like last time. I ran into him while grocery shopping one evening, and after chatting about being stuck in my writing, he gave me some great advice. He said he read somewhere that a lot of the greats, while writing, would never quit for the day at the end of a chapter or scene. Instead, they would stop on a really intense part, that way when they picked it back up, they'd resume during that exciting flow, when the words just fall right out of you. Trying it out, I wrote the final half of my book in mere weeks instead of months. Thank you, Zar!

There are a few very special author friends of mine I have to show major appreciation for. First and foremost, Lainey Reese. Woman, you called me a "top shelf, five-star author," and I just about fainted. To hear that from someone I admire as much as you…that's a top ten moment in this girl's LIFE. When I write the next one, my mantra will be, "Make Lainey proud."

Crystal Aurora Rose Reynolds, you couldn't read the love scenes in book 1, and you were scared to death to read book 2 because of the angst, but I'm so happy you finally dove in headfirst and ended up staying up all night because you couldn't put it down. That, to me, is quite an accomplishment. I'm so glad to share a wedding anniversary with a wonderful couple who also got their HEA. If that's not good juju, I don't know what is.

J.C. Cliff, I love you to the moon and back. That may be a lot of people's saying, but it's so true for us. Such a small world we live in, my cousin bringing us together to make our dynamic team. Thank you for all you do, even when it's just to do some mutual freak-outs.

Danielle Jamie, my Savannah, you never hesitate when it comes to being my partner-in-crime. Thank you for my beautiful chapter headings, for making me laugh constantly, and for being my pint-sized sidekick. Love you, woman.

Belle Aurora, thank you for your critical eye. Focusing not only on the story itself but also my writing, it meant the world to me when you said I've "taken to writing like it's second nature." You were one of the first authors I ever pimped on my Kayla the Bibliophile page nearly three years ago, were one of the first authors I edited for Hot Tree a year later, and are one of the first people I turn to when I need writing advice. You are so special to me <3

Sommer Stein with Perfect Pear Creative Covers,

thank you so much for my beautiful book! You work hard to give your authors exactly what they envision, but give great advice when it's needed. There's no one else I recommend more.

Anni and Brittany, you're in the book. Obviously, I love ya asses.

Finally, and most importantly, Jason, Josalyn, and Avary, my world. Thank you for being so proud of me. Not a day goes by when one of you girls don't tell a complete stranger, "My mommy is an author," with looks of pride and wonder on your perfect little faces. Jason even has the timekeeper at work reading his wife's hard work. It's empowering and so motivating knowing y'all are behind me. I love you three more than anything in this entire world.

For my readers, thank you for 'getting' me. That makes this extroverted introvert super-nerd veddy veddy happeh.

Songs included in chapter titles:

Sia - Chandelier
Killswitch Engage - End of Heartache
Hender - Lips of an Angel
Christina Aguilera - Just a Fool
Blake Sheldon - Lonely Tonight

Made in the USA
Coppell, TX
11 July 2021